The Gordian Knot

The Gordian Knot

JoAnn Fastoff

VANTAGE PRESS
New York

This is a work of fiction. Any similarity between the names and characters in this book and any real persons, living or dead, is purely coincidental.

Cover design by Susan Thomas

FIRST EDITION

Published by Vantage Press, Inc.
419 Park Ave. South, New York, NY 10016

Manufactured in the United States of America
ISBN: 0-533-14876-6

Library of Congress Catalog Card No.: 2004091118

0 9 8 7 6 5 4 3 2

To A.J. and Sweetness

Preface

1980

(Dasht-e-Kavir, a remote desert 200 miles southeast of Tehran)

The night of April 24, eight American servicemen died when their helicopter and a transport plane collided as they were leaving a refueling area after their operation had been called off. . . .

"A knot so involved as not to be easily unraveled."
—Webster's Unabridged Dictionary

. . . Pentagon officials, including the senior military officer who briefed reporters, refused to discuss details of the plan beyond the point where it was aborted in the darkness of the Iranian desert. However, other sources revealed the helicopters were to have taken commandos to a landing area near Tehran where the raiders would have linked up with waiting vehicles that would drive them through the city. With darkness as their ally, the commandos were to surprise and overcome the Iranian Fundamentalist students at the American Embassy, locate and round up the 50 hostages held there, and then speed to an airstrip outside the city to board a waiting transport plane.

But something went wrong.

Before the mission could begin, one helicopter developed spiraling problems. A plane's hydraulic system went awry and the plane could not get off the ground. Disaster struck. The rotor of the other helicopter sliced into a transport plane. Both exploded. Ammunition aboard both planes started exploding, lighting up the desert night like the Fourth of July. Only one man aboard the transport plane could be rescued. Five others on the ground were badly burned. Eight were killed.

Acknowledgments

Thank you, Bill Britt, for understanding my dilemma and jumping in; Detective Frank Lewark, Westminster, Colorado Police Department; my husband, Robert Aulston, for his incisive and unbiased view of the legal system; Robert Guthrie, U.S. Attorney General's Office, Denver, Colorado; Bill Shriver for his creative "Point" knowledge; Sandy Scarborough for her medical imagination; my wonderful dear Vietnam buddies: Dick Simmons, Al Binder, Dennis Betts, Dale Jackson and Dan Salin; my parents Norman and Sarah Fastoff for saying I had it in me all the time; and of course, You, God, for waking me from the dream.

All my love Ang and Dave,
—JAF

The Gordian Knot

1

Five Years Later: Chicago, Illinois

Carl Sunderland was frantic. The speedometer read 90 mph, then 95. When it reached 100 he decided to slow down. "No sense in killing myself before I reach FBI headquarters," he muttered. He noticed a green van behind him. After many miles he finally acted on the suspicion that he was being followed. He pulled into a 7-Eleven store parking lot to use the phone. He called the number on the card. It was an FBI agent named John Mason.

"I have urgent information for Mason and only Mason," he told the secretary who answered the call.

"Mr. Mason is still on vacation, like I told you yesterday, sir," she said. "He won't be back until Monday."

This was Thursday, so Sunderland left a phone number and hung up. When he returned to his car he noticed that the green van that had been following him was nowhere in sight. He felt uneasy but drove off, his tires screeching. Minutes later he became aware of a faint hissing sound coming from the back seat. He pulled over to the shoulder of the road. As he turned his head to check on the sound, his car exploded, throwing him through the back window. He was killed instantly.

30 days later

John Mason was in his car and on his way home. He didn't know why, but he was suddenly struck with the memory of Carl Sunderland's funeral. Carl's ex-wife, Joan, although divorced from Carl for three years, had been distraught. John remembered holding her hand throughout the service. He was relieved when it was finally over.

He noticed through the car window that it was starting to rain. He was driving on a somewhat deserted stretch of highway and the darkness of the electrical storm and the hard rain bothered him. He squinted. As he turned on the car radio for a weather report he noticed up ahead a green van pulling out into the intersection, and then stopping! John pressed his hand on the car horn and didn't let up. He put his foot on the brake . . . it didn't work! He bit his bottom lip. He swerved to avoid colliding with the van but ran off the shoulder of the highway and down a steep embankment. His car turned over twice, breaking John's neck and killing him instantly. The green van waited a moment, and then drove off.

It was a dreary day for a funeral. They were putting John Mason, his father, into the ground. Mark thought about how his dad had warned his mom of his possible death. How had he known that he might die? His thoughts were mixed with anger and sadness. He felt he was now supposed to carry on for his father, but he was only a kid. How could he do that?

Mark, a slim boy, was crowned with short, wavy hair. Highly intelligent for ten years old, he was aware of this fact and his attempt at making friends his own age had been difficult at times. Nevertheless he tried hard. He tightened his clutch on his mother's hand and looked into her eyes. He looked away quickly because he knew that if his eyes lingered, they would be swimming in tears and he couldn't let his mother see him cry or she would break down.

Carol Mason glanced down at her son and wondered how she could possibly live without her husband. John had been a good husband and a great father. He was an FBI agent who had died in a car accident. Carol knew in her heart that he had been murdered, and by someone he knew. She would not stop until she found out by whom and why. His colleagues had assured her that the "Bureau" would investigate the accident, but she knew it would be half-hearted. Carol somehow suspected everyone, but she didn't know why.

Her slim body was tired and she was angry with her husband for dying so young. Unaware that she was standing in a trance-like state, she heard her mother's voice.

"Carol, it's time to go!"

The crisp voice of Linda Frazier, Carol's mother, had brought her back to the funeral. It was over. Her husband (her best friend) had been buried.

Linda Frazier was a beautiful woman. Her silvery hair was hiding beneath a large black hat. She glanced over at her daughter, and knowing what it felt like to be a widow, imparted sage advice. "You know," her mother continued, "you must go on. John would be upset if he knew you were depressed."

"Grandmother, Mom's gonna cry," Mark whispered in her ear.

"Mark," the regal lady continued, "we have to keep going, and we will keep your father's memory alive by going on. The worst thing about mourning the dead is being dead yourself, when you're alive." Mark thought about his grandmother's words and knew they were true. Even at 10 years old, he knew she was right.

Carol and Mark would move from Chicago to Washington, D.C., where Carol's mother and three brothers still resided. Carol felt that she and her son could start over in a different city. She would return to teaching and Mark would receive a well-rounded education in the nation's capital. Most of all she knew she couldn't stay in the same city where her husband had been killed.

"Carol, let's go!" her mother repeated with a bit of frost in her voice. "You and Mark need to pack so we can go home to D.C. together."

Carol was miffed. "No, Mother," she replied. "We will meet you at the end of the school year like we discussed. There are a lot of things I must settle for John, and there are other things I must settle for myself. Besides, it's only six weeks away. Don't worry."

Carol trembled when the black limousine pulled up. As she and Mark walked toward the long, black car, she glanced back, for the last time, at her husband's grave.

The weeks passed. Gradually, but finally, Carol and Mark were starting to exhale. They were actually looking forward to the move. Although usually tidy, Mark's room was filled to the brim with boxes and luggage. He took a quick look around his bedroom the last night he was to sleep in it and spied the baseball glove his father had given him. He was told that his Grandfather Will had given it to his father. Will had once told him that he had worn this glove in left field in the old "Negro Leagues." He loved to tell the story that he could have beaten Jackie Robinson into the Major Leagues, but by the time the leagues had become integrated, he was too old to play baseball professionally. Mark would listen to those old stories over and over.

He smiled as he held the memory of his Grandfather Will's stories in his heart, now never to be told again. Grandfather Will had died the year before. Now Mark looked at the glove with new respect because Will had given his father the only thing that meant something to him. Now the glove was his to keep.

"You hold on to this glove, son," Mark's father used to say to him. This was the glove Mark kept beside his bed. This was the glove that reminded him how much his father loved him.

Mark glanced around the room once more like a spotlight searching for a plane in trouble. He spotted it—an old army duffel bag. His father had told Mark that it was a lucky bag, and that he had slept on it during the Vietnam War. Because of this bag, he was never seriously hurt or wounded. John would tell Mark that this bag would always keep him safe. Mark would smile, as he was doing now, because he wondered how an old army duffel bag would keep him safe.

It was the end of the school year and Mark had advanced to the sixth grade. He watched his mother pack.

Carol and John's bedroom was also cluttered with boxes and luggage for the move to D.C. Carol looked at her husband's clothes and wondered what she would do with them. The room was drenched in sunlight due to the absence of drapes, and the clutter seemed to assist the dust in throwing off a dreamy-foggy appearance. Carol packed slowly. She dreaded this part of the move because she had to decide on what to do with the voluminous memorabilia left by her deceased husband. As she plopped down on the edge of the bed she spied something hanging in the closet. It was John's college letter sweater.

1969: Champaign, Illinois

Carol had been a student at the University of Illinois for five months, and because the school was so large, was sure she would never get the opportunity to meet a man, much less date one. But one morning, as she was rushing to her first class on her bike, she was barely paying attention when she struck a pedestrian and knocked him down, sending his books in numerous directions. Overwhelmed with embarrassment, she helped the young man get up from the ground.

He shrugged it off as Carol finally calmed down enough to meet his eyes. She shivered. He was so handsome, and in a letter sweater, he made her stutter. She helped him pick up his books (all eight of them), and wondered why he had so many.

"I'm returning these to the library for my frat brothers," he said. "By the way," he continued, "aren't you going to apologize for almost making me a gimp, or at the very least join me for coffee?" He then extended a hand. "My name is John Mason," he said with a twinkle in his eye.

Although she didn't drink coffee, she blurted out the words "Oh yes!" then caught how stupid she must have sounded, and blushed. John remarked that it was refreshing to see a woman blush, and she was really on fire then. Her freckles seemed to take on a hue of their own. "I'm Carol Frazier," she said in between hot flashes.

They wound up cutting classes for the day and spent it talking. She loved his large physique. He loved the way she walked. She thought his hazel eyes were beautiful against his dark brown skin. When he smiled, his dimples seem to make his face sparkle. *I'm in love,* she thought. He thought she had the prettiest legs he'd even seen. In praising her he made her blush even more.

Over the next several months they learned a lot about each other. Although she felt John was somewhat arrogant, Carol also believed he was honest. He was in his senior year at Illinois and she was a freshman. He was majoring in criminal law and was already accepted at Northwestern University Law School, located in a northern suburb of Chicago. She wanted to teach. He wanted to eventually become an FBI agent and she was thrilled. He was 21 and she was 18. Their first cup of coffee ended their single lifestyles.

Carol's three brothers seemed stumped when she started dating John, as they had never realized their sister had ANY taste in men. This man they approved of unanimously. John, an only child, felt comfortable with the Fraziers, and her parents liked him as much as she did. Whenever the two were angry with each other, John would still go ahead and play basketball with Carol's brother Ron, also a senior at Illinois. Sometimes John and Ron would go to the movies or a sports event without her, and this would make her bristle. Ron and John would chuckle. John knew that if he hung around Ron or talked with any member of Carol's family on the phone, she'd hear about it, especially if she was mad at him.

When her father, Larry, died of a heart attack at the end of her sophomore year, John—by that time heavily involved in law school exams—felt he could not get away to attend the funeral in Washington, D.C. Carol was depressed. Although John was now on a different college campus, it was still only a three-hour train ride, so they were able to visit each other most weekends. Albeit she was only going to be away from school for a week, without John it seemed after two days that she had already been gone a month. He obviously felt the same way, because on the day of the funeral as they were lowering Larry Frazier's body into the ground, a cab pulled up and John alighted. They embraced without concern for the onlookers, as she knew they were truly in love.

Carol's mother told John to make sure there was always communication. "Talk to each other like Larry and I did," she said. Carol always remembered how serious her mother was when she said it. She also never forgot that her mother displayed an elevated deportment throughout the ordeal of her father's untimely death, and that she felt proud to be her daughter.

The ringing of the telephone brought her back to the present. She answered the phone and spoke with her cousin Jerry. She looked at John's clothes again and decided to offer them to Jerry, who accepted graciously. Carol and Mark were almost packed and ready for travel.

"D.C. is a great place, honey," she explained to her son. "It has a river and museums and parks."

Mark replied that Chicago had a lake and museums and parks too. She knew that he didn't want to leave Chicago, but if she stayed, she would always be reminded that Chicago was the city in which her husband had died. She couldn't believe that her husband was dead! He was only 37 years old, with a lot of life to live. She kept telling herself that he hadn't died in vain. There had to be an outside cause for his death and she was going to find it!

John Mason had been an FBI agent for over 10 years. He had told Carol and Mark that there were elements relating to his line of work that he couldn't discuss with them. It was part of his job not to discuss. "You don't need to know them anyway, Carol," he would say. He had been working on a case that had consumed his last 30 days. He hadn't been himself, he had been abnormally preoccupied. He was involved in something that had completely overtaken him. He wasn't talkative any longer, and he wasn't John any longer. He had mentioned to Carol on several instances that if anything were to happen to him, she and Mark were to go to Washington, D.C., where they would be safe. They were to locate Howard Watson; John said they could surely trust Howard.

Mark thought about his father's last days and recalled how worried his mother had become. Now he realized that she was starting to believe his father had been murdered.

Carol wondered why they had to get to Howard Watson, and why hadn't Howard Watson attended John's funeral? She recalled how many times John had written about him in his letters from Vietnam, how many times he had mentioned Howard and their Academy days, and how many times Howard had apologized over and over again about not making it to their wedding because he was on assignment in a remote part of Colombia. She had never met him but she knew that Howard had been important to John's life. But WHERE WAS HE? She had sent him a telegram and left a detailed message with his service regarding John's death and subsequent funeral. But—no Howard! Finally, after several calls to his home, she called the FBI Headquarters in Washington, D.C. and was informed that Howard Watson was on assignment in Russia. Carol felt this was a bad omen.

The "Bureau" told Carol that John had died in a car accident, "his brakes had gone out." Carol knew that was too coincidental. *What was John working on that took his life?*

She packed the last of their clothes and called her mother and brothers to inform them of their flight and arrival times. "I don't want to look back, Mother. I love you." She hung up the phone.

The next morning mother and son took a cab to the airport. She stared out the window at the beautiful city of Chicago where her son had been born, and where her husband had died. She didn't ever want to come back.

Mark grew impatient. It seemed like hours before their plane was to take off. Ten minutes before flight time they boarded the plane. As they arrived at their seats, the boy screamed, "Mom, I left my army bag in the airport! I can't go without Dad's lucky bag!"

With that, he ran off the plane with baseball glove in tow. Carol gasped. She grabbed her purse, the carry-on luggage and ran after her son in a frenzy.

Mark ran through the airport until he glimpsed sight of the bag still lying on the chair in the restaurant where he had left it. Carol caught up to him completely out of breath, ready to scold him when he started to cry. "Mom, I'm sorry. But I only have a few things of Dad's and I just couldn't leave this bag."

Carol suddenly realized that her son had been suffering silently and probably for her sake. She grabbed him and held him tightly. They sat on a bench quietly for a couple of minutes as they watched their plane take off without them and then, seconds later . . . burst into flames.

2

The police retained them for 24 hours. Because they had left the plane at the last minute, and were the only survivors, it was very suspicious. Eventually the police and the FAA concluded that Carol and Mark had had nothing to do with the explosion and that they were lucky to have gotten off. She, too, realized that they were lucky indeed. She also felt in the back of her mind that their lives were in danger. The FAA informed Carol that an investigation was underway, but if she and Mark felt safe in continuing their journey to the nation's capital, they were by all means free to go. She called her mother to tell her what had occurred. Milton, her oldest brother, a physician, answered the phone.

"Milt, this is me," she said.

"Where the hell have you been, Carol?" Milton shouted into the phone.

"Milt, listen to me! Where is Mother? I don't want her to know what has happened."

"Carol, she knows," he reported reluctantly. "Listen, Sis, I'm coming to get you two . . ."

But before Milton could finish his sentence she interrupted with "No, Milt, we'll be fine. Tell Mother we'll take an early bus tomorrow morning." Having said that, she hung up. Milton stared at the phone for what seemed like hours as he was faced with the responsibility of telling his mother his sister's decision.

Carol wanted to get out of Chicago as quickly as possible, before anything else could happen, and before the media realized she and Mark had been last minute cancellations. After giving the police her mother's phone number in D.C. (for any further information that might be necessary), they left.

They stayed overnight at a motel near the bus station. As their luggage was aboard the plane that had exploded two days prior, their only source of clothing at this time was changes of underwear, socks and toiletries packed in their carry-on luggage, which Carol kept near her at all times. She washed her blouse and Mark's shirt in the sink in the motel bathroom. They slept lightly. The next morning they arrived at the Greyhound Bus Station early enough to catch their 6:00 A.M. bus.

While traveling through Gary, Indiana, Carol's eyes moved about the bus. She was overwhelmed with anxiety. She glanced nonchalantly to the back of the bus and was surprised to see two well-dressed men pretending not to look at her. One was an FBI agent who had been a close friend of her husband. She decided not to strike up a conversation with them unless they approached her, as she didn't want to do anything out of the ordinary or make herself obvious. She concluded that the Bureau had dispatched two agents to guarantee their safety to D.C. and she felt somewhat relieved. She took a quick peek at Mark, who was asleep. She then felt secure enough to close her eyes. She thought about absolutely nothing for a full moment, then drifted into a needed sleep.

Summer, 1964: Washington, D.C.

"But Mom!" thirteen-year-old Carol wailed. "Why can't I run track? Ron does!"

She wanted to run track at school like her older brother Ron, but hit an impasse with her mother refusing to sign the authorization allowing her this extracurricular activity.

"Because, young lady," Linda Frazier responded, "you're a girl, and girls should be . . ."

"Playing a piano, cooking in some kitchen, or saying 'yes, sir' to their husbands!" Carol broke in.

Linda Frazier was steaming. She glanced over at her husband Larry, for assistance and was stunned by his statement.

"Linda, if Carol wants to run track, play football or climb Mt. Fuji, what do we care?"

She shot her husband a look that made him shrink. He became mute. But, Linda actually felt her husband was right. It was a different era and women were wearing mini-skirts, working in formerly "men-only" segments of industry, and bringing in their own paychecks. She had to concede to the new time, no matter how much she disliked the results.

"Okay, Carol, but when you get hurt, don't come crying to me, because I told you so!"

Father and daughter laughed loudly, requiring Linda to re-examine her statement and then to subsequently laugh the loudest.

13

Spring, 1966, Washington, D.C.

Carol had been training for a bike/run biathlon race to benefit leukemia research, and although he was only fourteen, her younger brother Bill, was her trainer. As she was nearing the end of the bike portion of her training, a young man, biking toward her, and perhaps glancing at her beauty instead of the road ran into her, knocking her off her bike. As she hit the pavement, the handlebar crushed into her right shoulder, breaking her collarbone and rendering her helpless in getting up. She could hear several voices talking, but she couldn't open her eyes. She remembered that her body felt as if it was on fire. Before losing consciousness she heard Bill asking, "Carol, are you okay? Sis, are you okay?"

The bike remained in the Frazier's basement, untouched, for the next three years.

"Indianapolis! Indianapolis, next stop!"

The sound of the bus driver's voice woke Carol and Mark abruptly. She hadn't realized she'd been asleep, but she figured it had been about three hours, because her 5'8" frame felt stiff from non-movement. In Indianapolis, the bus driver informed the passengers that there would be a twenty-minute stop. Carol decided to call her mother.

Linda Frazier expected to hear from her daughter every time the bus stopped. She was quite relieved when Carol mentioned that the Bureau had dispatched two agents (one of whom she knew) to watch out for her and Mark.

"I still want you to call—okay, Carol?"

She hung up the phone and watched Mark exit the station's store with a large chocolate bar. She waved to him to hurry it along. As they walked toward their bus, the two FBI agents approached them. One of them, David, said he had to talk to her. He said it was a matter of life and death. Fear ran through her body and it froze the blood in her veins. She tried to be calm but couldn't help blurting out, "David, what is happening to us?"

He grabbed her shaking body and tried to calm her down. "Carol, I don't know, but John told me some harm might come to you and Mark if something fatal happened to him."

"He told you that?" she asked.

"Yes," David replied. "You and Mark will need protection on your way to D.C. You *are* going to D.C., aren't you, Carol?"

She said yes, to which David replied that he and the other agent would drive them. It would be the only way to guarantee their safety. She felt grateful and decided to call her family to tell them of the change in plans. David asked that she not make the call until they reached Cincinnati. Carol looked at the other agent, who hadn't said a word throughout the whole conversation. She felt uneasy. She didn't trust him, but she didn't know why.

While she and Mark retrieved their luggage, the two agents rented a car from a lot across the street from the bus station. The four people got into a late model sedan and rode through Indianapolis.

Except for the intermittent reminiscing with David about his and John's initial meeting at the FBI Academy, no one really had anything to say. But once they reached Cincinnati, David, who was driving, looked in his rearview mirror and asked Carol, who sat in the backseat with the other agent, "Do you know where the tape is?"

Without taking her eyes from the window, Carol answered, "What tape?"

He stared a moment but continued, "Didn't John give you a tape to take to D.C.?"

She was puzzled. "No, David, I don't know about any tape."

David tried to appear undisturbed by the news. He looked over at Mark, who sat in the front passenger seat and asked half-jokingly, "He didn't give you the tape, did he, buddy?"

The boy said, "Nope, my dad only gave me his lucky duffel bag and my grandfather's baseball glove."

"Maybe we got our wires crossed," David said. Carol thought deeply about the conversation which had just taken place. She thought about it all the way to Dayton, where they stopped for lunch.

The travelers pulled into a "Mom and Pop" diner off the highway. Once they had eaten, Mark felt he couldn't go any further without rest. "David, we must stop." Carol half-pleaded. "Mark needs rest and we've been up since 4:00 A.M." She looked at her watch and noticed it was 3:00 P.M. The week's events certainly contributed to his being drained. She felt that her 10-year-old boy was becoming a man way before his time.

"That sounds good, Carol," David replied. All this time the other agent had still not uttered a word. This made Carol extremely concerned about her and her son's safety. They drove past two "dives" before Mark yelled that up ahead was a Holiday Inn. All agreed to stop, and David pulled the car into the motel parking lot.

Carol hadn't realized that her and her son's room was next door to the agents' room until around 6:30 A.M. when she was awakened by conversation. Although she and Mark had been asleep for more than 10 hours, she was still dead tired and started to doze off again when she heard the words "Mason" and "accident." She put her ear to the wall to hear more talking but couldn't make out complete sentences. It was then that she decided that she and Mark

16

would leave the motel as soon as possible, without telling the men. She picked up the phone near the bed, stared at it for a moment, but then replaced it in its cradle.

By 7:00 A.M. they had dressed, packed their belongings and were on their way out the door when David knocked. Noticing that they were already dressed he asked her where they were going.

She replied that they were on their way to breakfast and the reason they had their luggage was because it contained all they had in the world and she didn't want it stolen.

He seemed pleased with her answer, but responded facetiously, "Well, let's go to breakfast then, shall we?"

The diner at the motel, although clean, was deserted. Breakfast was quiet, except for the occasional laugh and banter between Mark and David. The other agent, Eric (*finally, his name,* she thought) ate quickly then drifted over to the car to wait for them. David mentioned that Eric was not feeling well which explained why he'd been so quiet.

Carol was afraid of Eric. He had worn dark glasses the previous day, said very little, if anything at all, and put his hand on his gun, hidden beneath his jacket, more than once. When breakfast was concluded, she called her mother, who was away from home at a church function. Her brother Bill answered the phone. She informed him of the day's events regarding the two agents who were accompanying them to D.C. Bill wanted to know if Carol felt it would be safe to continue with them. Carol hesitated in answering but said, "Yes, Bill, and please look for us to arrive this evening."

The four people returned to the car where Carol was once again relegated to the back seat. She recalled the numerous times her husband had told her in his horrible fake Jamaican accent, "Bewa de parson who wea de dawk

17

glasses." She remembered laughing at this saying, but laughter was the last thing on her mind right now. She was of the belief that the reason an agent wore dark glasses was to look obscure and inconspicuous—but *at night?*

As the car proceeded on Interstate 70 east, her long body was becoming increasingly uncomfortable in the backseat. Finally they arrived in Columbus. While keeping an eye on the road, David turned to Carol and asked the same question, "Where's the tape?"

It dawned on her that he was serious. Before she could answer, Eric pulled the gun from his jacket and put it to her side.

"We want the tape," he said gruffly, "or we will hurt you!"

Carol stared blankly for a moment then asked, "What has happened to you, David?" But before he could answer he drove through a red light.

"Man, what are you doing?" Eric yelled. "We just went through a fuckin' red light!"

"Cool down, man," he replied. "It's a Sunday, and this is a little hick town."

"This little *hick* town is Columbus, Ohio," Eric quickly retorted.

Mark became startled. Carol said to him in a tight voice, "If anything happens to me, honey, you try to get to D.C. You can do it, I know you can."

"Shut up, Carol!" David shouted. His manner was terrifying. When the car slowed for another red light Carol screamed, "Mark, get out of the car! Now!"

The boy didn't hesitate. He threw his duffel bag into David's face and the car went out of control and hit a fire hydrant. Eric's gun went off and Carol slumped into the seat. The boy looked at his mother's limp body and knew she was dead. Then something occurred to him: he would be killed too, if he didn't get out of the car. In what seemed like slow motion, he grabbed his baseball glove and jumped from the car. Before David could open his door to run after him, a police car pulled up beside them.

Mark ran away into the maze of homes and trees nearby.

3

Mark had been traveling about an hour on the road. He was in silent, tearless shock as he headed toward Washington, D.C. It was a warm day and the sun was shining which prompted him to stop, sit on the side of the road and to think about what had happened. After awhile he reluctantly got up again and walked tiredly down the road until a car stopped, and the driver, a woman, asked if he needed a ride. He thought about his father's constant lectures on not hitchhiking and not picking up hitchhikers, because it was always bad news to hitchhike. "Most of the people are probably good people who just want to give someone a ride," he would tell Mark. "But there's always the jerk who turns out to be the kidnapper, the thief, the murderer."

Mark remembered his father saying it was best not to hitchhike, to avoid becoming a statistic.

He politely refused the ride and the lady asked how far he was going. He answered that he was going to Washington, D.C. "Honey, you're goin' the wrong way," the woman explained in a southern drawl. "You're gonna hafta go back up to I-70 EAST. Do you wanna ride, cause I'm going that way?" They were in Hillsboro, Ohio, about 280 miles west of Washington, D.C. Although it was getting dark, Mark said no.

The woman shook her head from side to side and drove off.

As Mark trudged on, numerous drivers stopped him

on the road to ask if he was lost or needed a ride. He continued to say "No," to both questions. Out of fear, whenever he spied a police car, he would hide in the bushes or behind trees. He walked as far as he could but was soon too weary to walk and sat on the ground behind a grove of trees. He soon dozed off.

3 years earlier, Chicago, Illinois

"But Mom, all my friends have brothers and sisters. . . ."

Mark had been born in Chicago and when he turned two, his father was transferred to the Trace Element Unit of the FBI in Philadelphia. Two years later, the family was transferred back to Chicago. Although he enjoyed his parents' company immensely, he longed for a brother or sister, preferably a brother. His mom would often explain to him that she couldn't physically have any more children. "Remember my operation?" she would tell him. She would also counter his pleas by telling him that perhaps he should visit his pals more often and find out how they felt about their sisters and brothers. Nonetheless, Mark's longing did not cease.

He was tall for his age. He was over five feet tall, at only 10 years old. The doctors told his parents that he would be tall because they were tall. He was thrilled to be taller than most of his classmates. It made him feel superior. His dimples, though, seemed to give away his age, because they made him look pixieish; at least that was his mother's description. His dark brown, wavy hair was always worn short because he could brush it in a matter of seconds and be done with it. He derived great pleasure piecing together 1,000-piece puzzles and Erector sets. He was one of the smartest kids in his class and an enthusiastic member of the track and Little League baseball teams. He vividly recalled when his mom would kiss him at night, that she would always step on some of the pieces of the Erector set, forgotten on the bedroom floor. He would cringe in his bed because she seemed to find pieces with her feet *in the dark* that he couldn't find in the light.

Mark believed he had to be first in everything to get ahead. He wanted to be an engineer because he thought engineers contributed the most to the world, and that they could build and draw things that would be important for people. John was pleased that his son had made a good choice, and that although he knew he would probably change his mind a dozen times regarding a career path, he felt Mark at least seemed to be learning to be his own man. Father and son would argue often about the news and sports. Sometimes Mark would be right, and this would irritate John. "How dare that little twerp be right?" he would tell his wife, with a smile.

The sun and the sound of a cow woke him up. He got up, peed on the tree and started walking again. When he had been on the road close to an hour, he became aware that he was in the state of Maryland. The several hundred square miles where Maryland, Virginia and West Virginia merge were laden with endless rolling hills. Every once in a while he ventured into a thicket of trees for shade or shelter. It was then that he would see other roads, the kind that were visible for only a few yards as they wound their way up distant hills and into groves of pines. To someone else, it was probably yet another man-made blemish in the wilderness. In Mark's eye the curve of a one-lane road hidden in the trees was the beckoning arm of adventure. "Some other time," Mark muttered out loud. "I've got enough adventure on my hands for now, thanks."

While the mystery roads on his right always came and went in a variety of shapes and sizes, he usually kept his eye on the reliable concrete serpent, Interstate 70. *Stray from that baby*, he thought, *and you're trapped in the TWILIGHT ZONE . . .*

"This is scary, and I'm STUPID LEE JAGGER," he declared aloud, to absolutely no one. Just hearing himself say that name brought an involuntary grin to his face. It was his dad's reference to what he had always called "Another-Big-Lipped-Rock-Star-Getting-Paid-to-Act-Black." No. He wasn't afraid of the countryside. He was bored with it.

"It can't stay boring forever," Mark said to the sky. He was thinking about a movie he had recently watched with some boys from his school. In the movie, a car full of teenagers was traveling along a highway when the highway started coming up from the ground. The teenagers started screaming and the highway swallowed them and their car. "Just like that hallway in *Poltergeist*," he said aloud.

All of a sudden the highway became the major focus of his attention. The view was hill after hill of oak and pine trees, fruit orchards and miles of barbed wire fences protecting property and cattle. Mark's eye suddenly spied a state police car moving in the opposite direction to which he was traveling. He looked down the steep shoulder of the highway and noticed the terrain was soft dirt and knee-high grasses alongside the highway. Ahead was a weed-infested trench. Somewhere hidden in its center (where the mosquitoes gathered) was a stream. He had to disappear from the road—now!

He realized he was thirsty when he noticed the mosquito-laden stream. It was hardly appealing, but using his baseball glove as a sword, he took a deep breath and swatted as many of the little buggers as he could. He drank quickly. He then scrambled up the bank and burst through the remainder of the tall grass and emerged once again near the highway. The police car was nowhere in sight. He exhaled.

Although he had logged plenty of car trips to the nation's capital, none of this looked familiar to him. In fact, he thought, it looked like another planet. Instead of seeing the countryside whiz past his backseat window at 60 miles per hour, he was imagining himself in the middle of a typically miserable Cub Scout hike. The only difference was The Road. The Interstate. Always in sight. *It has to be,* he thought. How else was he going to have any idea of where he was if he couldn't see the huge green highway signs that spelled out the towns and their distances?

A car pulled alongside him. Mark suffered a brief blur of vision. "Oh God" he said aloud. He snapped his head sharply to the left and locked eyes with . . . *please just let it be a nosy driver . . . please let it be . . . Oh God,* he thought. He had never seen a face like it before. It was yellow. It was covered from forehead to chin with brown, matted hair. Fiery bloodshot eyes with coal-black pupils bore into his baby-browns. Their eyes connected but the car coasted past him. The few inches of visible flesh seemed to float across the man's face and head. Mark had frozen in his tracks.

The teenage driver then pulled off his mask, laughing in gulps. Two teenaged girls emerged in their seats laughing as hard. Mark then watched the small car drift into the far-left lane, accelerate, and then disappear over the hill in the distance. He pointed his glove in the car's direction, whispered the magic command and *Blam!* the car exploded like a "Death Star."

He reached the shade and security of another tree and leaned against it, panting for breath. The sun was now very hot. He remembered a car trip in the past when he had asked his dad, "Why do they have dirt roads going across the highway?"

"Welllll," his dad had said, never taking his eyes off the road, "that's just in case an ambulance or tow truck needs to make a U-turn for some reason and head back the other way."

A few moments later he rounded a bend and stared straight into yet another ravine. The sound of the stream below was deafening. The alternative was walking on the shoulder of the highway and crossing the bridge. He glanced over his left shoulder to notice the highway was pretty empty. He clutched his glove with both hands and started across the bridge in a full run. He ran out of steam 150 yards later when he had crossed the bridge. The narrow pathway between the road and the bridge railing looked like a nightmare waiting to happen. He could just picture some carload of big kids playing a game of Let's-Drive-Real-Close-to-the-Little-Asswipe-and-See-if-He-Jumps. A tear rolled down his cheek before he realized he was crying. He also realized he was hungry.

His second day on the road. His second bridge, but not his last. The task of making his way across trenches and streams had become a nightmare, especially when he had to walk away from the highway to find a place safe enough to cross the larger streams. He would cross the bridges, but only when he had to, and certainly never without taking time out to find the biggest stick possible to carry with him. *That ought to be enough to scare off anyone,* he thought.

4

It was during one of those fast hikes across a long bridge that a woman driving a pickup truck edged over to the railing and stopped about twenty yards in front of him.

"Son," she said, "do you need a ride? How far ya goin'?"

Mark replied that he was going to Washington, D.C.

"Well, I'm going' to Monessen and that's about a three-hour drive. But you're welcome to ride with us," she offered. He was tired and hungry, and he noticed that the truck was full of fruit; he needed food and felt he had no real alternative.

Agnes Mobley and her two sons, Jerry and Timmy, were sitting in the front with their mother, but Agnes made the boys move closer to her so that Mark could fit on the seat. As far as Mark could determine, Jerry was about his age, and Timmy was probably a couple years younger. Agnes asked numerous questions: Where was he going, where were his parents, why was he by himself? He answered some of her questions. She wanted to know why a little kid was traveling by himself to Washington, D.C., on foot.

She continued asking him questions as he chomped on as many apples and peaches as he could. When he decided not to answer any more questions, she stopped asking.

It seemed that he had been in the truck only a very

short time when they reached Monessen, but in actuality it was about a three-hour trip. He had felt safe with this lady and her boys and the ride had taken his mind off everything that had happened to him.

Agnes finally, and reluctantly, had to tell Mark this was the end of the line. As she pulled into the Monessen bus station, she took two twenty-dollar bills out of her jeans pocket, stared at the money for a moment, and then handed them to him. She wrote her name and phone number on a piece of paper and told him to call her when he got to D.C.

"You don't have to say much." she said. "Just have your grandma tell me you've made it safely, that's all."

She then walked up to a window counter at the bus station, bought a one-way ticket to Washington, D.C., and showed him where to sit until they called his bus number. The bus wasn't due to leave for another thirty minutes so he hugged Jerry and Timmy, and finally, Agnes. She hugged him back and walked away. She turned briefly in his direction and wiped a tear from her eye before her sons could notice. She took a deep breath, felt reasonably sure that she had done the right thing, and left.

Once Agnes became a memory, Mark suffered a traumatizing flashback of the last bus ride in which two agents approached him and his mother. He felt nauseous. With forty dollars in his pocket, he went out the opposite door of the bus station and again headed for the Capital.

He'd been walking for about two hours when he started thinking that he was glad he hadn't taken the bus. He had walked another hour when he saw pears on a tree by the road. He picked off three and ate them quickly, not stopping to breathe. It dawned on him that he hadn't had a real meal all day. He fell asleep under an oak tree and hours later woke up to feel cool rain on his face. He climbed the tree and curled up his body in the giant branch to escape the dewy dampness of the ground.

Below him, sniffing the carpet of pine needles, was a deer. "It's only me," he said to the animal as he peered down at the deer. He watched as it lifted its head and then tilted it straight up until it was looking him in the eye. There wasn't a trace of fear or danger in the stares of either boy or animal. The deer folded its legs underneath its body and settled onto the bed of pines. Its body was indeed resting, but its mind was already programmed. Another boy Mark's age most likely would've made some distracting noise that would have sent the deer on its way in seconds. As he stared at the animal, Mark's mind opened itself to a flood of scenes that were only two years old. In the full minute that it took him to fall asleep, he remembered all the details of an entire day's worth of hunting that might have happened only yesterday.

2 years earlier: Forest Preserves outside Chicago

It was late fall and he and his dad were set to go on Mark's first hunting trip. He never once thought, even for a moment, that they would actually see a deer, much less kill one. But his dad was the person who killed it, and Mark remembered being mad at him for a whole week. He had felt sick to his stomach when the dying animal looked at him with glazed eyes. Then she was dead. He had been eight years old.

The rain stopped beating him like a cruel stepmother. The sun finally showed its cowardly head, once the rain had dissipated. The deer was gone. Mark climbed down from the tree and started walking again. He had passed the little towns of McConnelsburg and Cumberland, Maryland, when he spotted a 7-Eleven store. It was late evening so he bought dinner: microwave popcorn, a hamburger, a Coke, and a cherry pie. After eating in the store and using their bathroom, he started on yet another trek.

He politely refused ride after ride but finally became too tired to walk and decided to park himself under a tree on the other side of a fence. After removing his socks and shoes, he stared at the blisters on his feet. He noticed the sign, which read KEEP OFF—PRIVATE PROPERTY, but felt he could go no further. He threw his shoes, socks and baseball glove over the fence.

As he placed his hands on the fence to go over it, he was knocked two feet off the ground. *It was electrified!*

He gathered himself off the ground, walked down as far as he could, trying to reassure himself that the electricity had to end soon. He was right. The fence eventually became barbed wire and as he touched it gingerly, he was relieved to find it was not all-electric. In scaling it he was pulling his second leg over when it caught the wire and tore his pants, along with his leg. Blood oozed out rapidly, making Mark sick to his stomach. He had never seen this much blood before, and it was all coming from *him!*

He tried to clean the wound but his hands hurt badly. He then decided to use his shirt, but there was too much blood; he had to use his jacket. He was thinking that his mother would faint, just like she always did, if she saw this much blood coming from him.

Then he remembered his mother was *dead.*

His father was *dead.*

He was overwhelmed with loneliness. He started crying.

"God, did I do something wrong?" he said to the sky. "Why do you hate me so much?" He vowed that he would make it to his grandmother's house. Although it was quite warm during the day, as soon as the sun dipped beneath the horizon, it turned somewhat chilly. He bundled himself up in his bloody jacket and cried himself to sleep under another tree.

"Hey, boy! What're you doin?"

Mark woke up to look into two giant blue eyes staring at him. "Son, didn't you see the 'No Trespassing' sign?"

"Yes, sir," he replied, "but I was tired. I'm sorry, sir." Jacob Tryer was obviously annoyed, but then asked Mark if he was by himself, and he replied affirmatively.

Tryer immediately started in with a barrage of questions. "Where's your ma and pa?"

Mark replied that they were dead.

Tryer looked over at his teenage son, Isaac and both realized this kid wasn't joking. Tryer asked him where he was headed and Mark replied "Washington, D.C."

"ON FOOT?" Isaac blurted.

"It's the only way I have to get there," Mark replied.

Tryer then shocked Mark by saying, "Son, I'll take you about as far as I can, and that's Westminster, and I'll put you on a bus there. Let me and my son, Isaac, go get the truck. Don't go nowhere, ya hear?"

Mark didn't know what to think. His mind started racing. He thought the man was going to call the police. *What if they're two more FBI agents looking for me?* His mind went blank with fear. He ran. He got about a third of a mile down the road when he realized that he had left his baseball glove under the tree. He limped back. When he got closer to the tree, he saw the glove was gone. His heart sank.

"You looking for this, son?" Jacob Tryer asked, holding

up Mark's baseball glove. Mark replied with a nod of his head.

Tryer tossed the glove to him. "You don't want nobody helping you, we can see that," he said. "But let me give you some advice—stick to the freeway and you'll make it to D.C. mighty fine, okay?"

Mark smiled and limped off. Jacob and Isaac Tryer stared at him as he left. His feet were really starting to hurt badly, so much so that he had to carry his shoes. His heels were raw and blistered and his feet and hands were red and swollen.

He limped into Hagerstown, Maryland, where he found an old rooming house along the road. A sign on the door read ROOMS $15 A NIGHT. He looked at the house which reminded him of one he'd seen in a horror movie. "This looks like the house in *Psycho*," he said aloud. After checking the balance of his money, he finally got up the nerve and knocked on the door. A large woman appeared. "Can you tell me how far it is to Washington, D.C.?" he asked.

The woman glanced at his feet with raised eyebrows. "More'n a day if you're walkin."

"Lady, I'll wash your dishes, clean your rooms, take out the trash, anything, if you just let me sleep here for the night," Mark blurted. "I'll be gone so early in the morning you won't remember that I was here."

Clara Baumgarten smiled slightly and told him that she *did* have a load of trash he could take to the garbage out back, but "You'd better be gone in the mornin', I mean it."

Mark promised he would. The Victorian house had not been kept up from the outside, but the interior was clean and cluttered with history. There were many old but price-less-looking mementos scattered about. After about a half-hour of work, Mark was shown a room, and a bath-room, complete with a bathtub. Clara ran a very warm bath for him so he could soak his feet. His haggard little body stayed in the tub for over an hour.

When he completed his bath, he started toward his bed, but stopped. With some type of strategy Clara was unaware of, he checked the windows, closet and under the bed. She thought he acted very scared. "Are ya lookin' for someone?" she asked.

He replied, "No," and closed the door slowly in her face. He slept 10 hours. As it was late, she had decided she would call the police in the morning.

She was sipping coffee the next morning when Mark was on his way out the door. She stopped him.

"Ain't you gonna eat, son?" she asked.

He said he didn't have time and he had only a few dollars left and also didn't want to spend all his money so early in the day.

She insisted that he eat first so that he would have energy to make his walk. She fed him, saying, "You did such a great job on the trash that breakfast is on me!"

He ate a lot more food. He thanked her for the nice bed, bath and food and was on his way again.

She had asked him numerous questions, but he was too busy eating to reply. She hoped he would be all right. *He* hoped he was nearing the end of his journey.

She liked this kid. She waved as he limped away. He waved back. He liked her too.

As soon as he was out of sight, she called the Maryland State Police. She told them in which direction the boy was headed. The MSP said they would find him, and not to worry. After an hour, hearing nothing from the MSP, she called again. She insisted that something was wrong with the boy because he was wearing a jacket with what she thought were bloodstains on it, and he was only ten or eleven years old.

The police said they would look into it, and a couple of hours later, when they finally got around to checking out her story, Mark had already made it to the town of Brunswick, about 40 miles west of Washington, D.C. By that time, his feet hurt so badly he didn't know if he could go on.

He tried looking inconspicuous in Brunswick. While hiding out in some large bushes, he found, to his surprise, that the police were slightly smarter than he thought. Actually, he had become so exhausted that he had fallen asleep in the bushes that were located behind the gas station where the Brunswick police gassed up their cars. He was taken to the police station because he couldn't (or wouldn't) explain where he was from or why he was sleeping behind the gas station.

Jim Stanley, a rookie police officer, was typing a report when Mark entered escorted by two cops. Stanley took his name and address and proceeded to ask him questions concerning his parents. He examined the boy's clothes, which were covered with what he figured to be blood. Three or four other officers were milling about and Mark suddenly felt embarrassed about the condition of his feet and hands. Stanley, sensing that the boy had come through some type of ordeal, decided to take him into the medics' office to finish his questioning.

Mark explained to the medic the accidents regarding his leg and hands. The medic confirmed that the boy "would live" but that he was suffering from total exhaustion. Stanley felt he should ask him some more questions, but Mark no longer wanted to talk. Eventually the police officer made him realize that he was a friend and that he was there to help him.

"Son, I'm sorry that I have to ask you these questions," he lamented, "but I need to know what has happened to you; where are you coming from; where are you on your way?"

He looked directly into Jim Stanley's eyes.

"My mom and dad are dead," he said slowly. "My mom was killed a week ago in Columbus, Ohio, when some men we knew kidnapped us."

The officer looked curiously at him and recalled that on the previous day he had read in a *Crime Reports Bulletin* that a woman had been shot in Columbus, Ohio, and federal agents were to be notified if her son, who suddenly fit Mark's description, was found.

Stanley (he told Mark to call him Jim) asked him how his mother was killed and Mark replied that she was shot in a car they were riding in.

Stanley thought a minute.

"Sit tight," he told the boy. He then asked a fellow officer to watch the kid while he went into the captain's office.

"Captain, I think I found the little boy!" he exclaimed excitedly. "You know, the one that's related to that agent killed a couple of months ago in Chicago, and his wife who was shot last week in Ohio?"

The captain jumped from his chair. "You mean he's *here?*" Stanley nodded. The captain then leafed through some files on his desk and found the FAX that instructed officers to call FBI Headquarters in Washington, D.C., and ask for an FBI Agent named Howard Watson. The chief immediately placed the call to Watson.

5

Howard Watson had returned to Linda Frazier's house to let her know, in person, that "no news was still good news" regarding Mark's whereabouts. The grandmother became distraught. He held her hand as he continued to reassure her about Mark's fate, but Mrs. Frazier, apparently distracted, babbled on about John asking her to bake Mark's favorite cherry pie when he came to visit.

"We won't eat it until he gets here, and if he doesn't come . . ." she droned on.

Howard's thoughts were elsewhere; feeling somewhat useless in this family situation, he returned to FBI headquarters to see if any new developments had occurred and to try to sort out his next move.

Mark was afraid. He asked if the agents coming for him were the ones who had been in the car with him and his mother.

"Lord, no!" Stanley replied. "As a matter of fact, they caught those two in Columbus and they're in jail right now."

"Are you sure?" Mark asked.

"Yes," Stanley replied.

Mark looked away as if he didn't believe him. Stanley wondered how this little boy had managed to see his mother shot and still get from Columbus, Ohio to Brunswick, Maryland, *on foot.* Stanley thought that he'd better wait until he knew for sure if Carol Mason was still alive before he told Mark that his mother hadn't died in the car in Columbus. He carried Mark to the officers' lounge and let him lie down on the sofa. He told him that Howard Watson was coming from Washington to get him, and that he would be fine—that it was over.

Mark felt measurably better. Stanley covered him with a blanket and told him to nap, reassuring him that he would come and get him when Agent Watson arrived.

Howard Watson knew he couldn't make a move to locate Mark because now he didn't know which agents he could trust. He felt that if there were "rogue" agents responsible for John's death, Mark would be killed. John was already dead; Carol was lying in a hospital in Columbus, Ohio, in critical condition. Howard thought to himself, *My God, is the kid next?"*

He tried calming Carol's mother, envisioning for her a scenario in which her grandson was all right, alive, and near the highway somewhere, on his way to D.C. But Linda Frazier was too distraught to be encouraged. Her only daughter was lying near death in a hospital room in another state; her son-in-law was dead. She prayed to God that her only grandson was alive. Linda Frazier was the type of person who gave strength to others, and she was proud of that. But today neither her three sons nor her neighbors, nor the rest of her family could lift her from her depression. "It's been three days since we've heard from Mark," she said sadly.

It had also been three days since Carol was shot in the backseat of a car, and Columbus police had apprehended the FBI agents responsible. Now Linda needed more strength just to go on thinking that her grandson was alive.

She had been advised that her daughter should not be

transported from Ohio to D.C. until the doctors knew for sure that she could survive the trip. Linda protested. She felt that Carol would have a better chance if she could be at a hospital in D.C., near her family and friends who loved her. Linda and her son Milton decided they would fly to Columbus and have Carol sent to D.C. by helicopter, with Howard's assistance. Howard had been glad to assist the family, and thus Carol was moved to D.C.

At this point Howard was still busy trying to reassure Linda, Milton, Ron and Bill that Mark was okay. "Right now, he's not going to trust anyone, so he's probably walking. More than likely he's hiding from the police too because he doesn't trust them and that's why we haven't heard any reports of a missing kid fitting his description. He'll be here soon, folks, and don't worry, he'll have the tape."

Linda had not been completely listening until Howard mentioned the word "tape." Bill was the one who asked.

"What tape, Howard?"

Howard replied that John had given Carol, or possibly Mark, a tape to bring to him in case of John's death.

"That boy doesn't have anything with him!" Linda frantically blurted out. "He left his duffel bag in the car where they found Carol!"

"You mean he left that bag in the car?" Howard asked, astonished at this revelation.

"Yes," Bill admitted, almost apologetically. "We didn't mention it because the police told us they would mail it to us."

Howard told them that he had to send for the bag, and that it might contain clues about John's death. He also told them he could get it by courier the next day, as it wasn't being used for evidence in the shooting of Carol.

37

Satisfied that he had some information he could use, Howard left.

The duffel bag arrived the next afternoon at FBI Headquarters, and Howard dismissed the courier with a tip and carried the bag gently into his office as if it were an infant. He closed the door behind him, silenced the expensive desk radio and placed the bag on his desk. If it were another time, another place, a happier circumstance, he would have immediately loosened the drawstring and spilled the contents across the desktop. Instead, he sat in his plush leather chair, his hands in his lap, and stared at the green army bag, the remains (as far as he was concerned) of his closest friend, John Mason.

He recalled that this was John's lucky duffel bag. Everyone close to them knew that it had saved John's life on two occasions and Howard remembered both instances. Mark knew how much this bag had meant to his father and Howard couldn't imagine it being out of Mark's hands unless . . . Mark had thrown it at the driver, and that's how he managed to get away!

The voices that drifted down the hall outside the office door suddenly became mute as the sunlight on the office walls slid to the floor. Not surprisingly, Howard was elsewhere.

1973: Vietnam

John Mason's duffel bag was propped up in a barracks window, supporting John's head as he sat on a cot that somehow supported his 200-pound, 6'4" frame without the slightest sign of strain. For a while though, the cot had shaken because John was laughing at what he called his favorite source of humor: Howard's knack for discerning the insignificant and using it to his advantage. This time, the subject was a barracks window. It seemed the men were not pleased at the fact that part of Vietnam's nearly impenetrable jungles was simply too close to the area where they lay their heads at night.

"It doesn't make any difference which barracks we stay in," Howard was saying. "It's all gonna come down to the windows."

"What are you talking about?" John asked. Both feet were planted squarely on his cot, his back against the wall, the duffel bag headrest silhouetted against the blue of a bright and cloudless day.

"It's elementary, my dear Mason," Howard explained. "My window faces directly north. I have a view of the widest expanse of what little property we actually control in this hellhole. I have a wonderful view of the Northern Lights when they aren't blocked out by exploding shells and jellied gasoline, and," he said as he pointed his finger in the air, "I can also look out my window during the day and not have my line of vision blocked by the sun."

John, who always complained about the sun beating on his cot, was shaking the steel bed frame with laughter and never heard the blast of the mortar shell that hurled him, cot and all, across the room. He regained consciousness some five minutes later to find himself staring into his soon-to-be best friend's face. Howard and another officer, Louis Castro, waited for the medic's prognosis. They watched John's face come back to life, wrinkle by wrinkle. "If it hadn't been for that duffel bag, man," Howard grinned nervously, "the back of your head would be a pineapple by now."

Only superficially hurt, John grinned back, thankful to be alive.

Howard's grin turned into a smile. He realized how silly he must look, sitting at his polished executive desk, grinning at an old duffel bag. But the smile soon faded. What had gone wrong? What had John known that caused him to be killed? What was so important that the Bureau didn't want anyone else to know? He knew one thing for sure—it was damned important, whatever it was, and he was going to find out no matter how long it took. *First*, he had to find Mark.

He searched the duffelbag cautiously, trying not to miss anything, no matter how trivial, but there was nothing in the bag that seemed important. Before he put it aside, he remembered the zippered side pocket partially concealed by a Velcro flap. He slowly opened the flap, unzipped the pocket and peered inside. A small tape recorder lay in its pocket. He lifted the machine out and saw it contained a tape.

He rewound the tape and listened. *Kool and the Gang* on side one—good movin' music, but nothing to get excited about. The flip side was the same. He felt discouraged. He had counted on John's tape being in that bag. Now, as much as he disliked the thought of waiting, there was nothing else to do. He couldn't make a move, unless he was sure it wouldn't raise any eyebrows or prompt any questions at the Bureau.

John had made him promise only weeks before his death, that if anything were to happen to him, he would see that Carol and Mark were brought to D.C. safely. One of them, surely, would have evidence of what John believed was going on in the Bureau! Was this evidence what had him killed and injured his wife, and maybe his son?

So far I haven't kept my word on any of my promises, he thought. *I've got to get to that kid before* . . . he didn't go on

40

with his thought. He just couldn't get it out of his mind that John had been murdered. But why was Carol almost killed? Did she know something, too? John would not have told his family any Bureau business, especially information that could cause their deaths. *No, he thought; Carol was probably trying to protect Mark, and the gun went off and she got hurt in the process.* He was thinking that if Mark weren't found within twenty-four hours, he would scour the earth looking for him. Howard was so upset that he had not attended John's funeral or offered comfort to Carol and Mark that he was beside himself. He had been in a remote part of Russia when the news of John's death finally reached him. By the time he could get back to the States, his friend had been buried and his wife and son were already on their way to D.C. He owed them his protection and he was now at a point where he didn't care who got in the way, whether it was another agent or even the Director himself, he was going to find Mark, and he had better be alive!

Howard arrived at his office the next morning to startling news. "You don't have to worry any longer, Mr. Watson," his secretary exclaimed. "Mark Mason has been found!"

The blank look on his face made his secretary regurgitate more information. "The notice!" she stammered. "About the missing boy of that Chicago agent killed a couple of months ago?"

He became frantic. "Where is he?"

"He's in Brunswick, Maryland, about forty miles from here," she replied.

Within seconds Howard was on the phone to the Brunswick police and was immediately transferred to Jim Stanley. "Hold Mark there. I'm the only agent that can pick him up. Just hold him there!"

"Is there a problem?" Stanley asked. Howard replied that the boy's life was still in danger, especially since he could identify the men who kidnapped him and his mother. Howard said he would be in Brunswick within the hour and that he was grabbing a helicopter.

While Stanley briefed his captain and other officers on Mark's situation, a man quietly, but confidently, went to the front desk of the Brunswick Police Station, handed the desk sergeant his "Howard Watson" identification card and badge, and said he was there to pick up Mark Mason. The sergeant studied the identification card and said, "You sure made it here fast. Do you need to see Officer Stanley before you take the boy back to D.C.?"

The man answered, "No, the boy needs to get to his family. I'll talk with the officer mid-week."

"I'll go get the lad," the sergeant quipped.

The sergeant retrieved Mark from the officers' lounge, glanced over in the direction of the captain's office for a moment, but not wanting to prolong the boy's need to get to his family, released Mark to "Agent Watson."

Fifteen minutes later, the meeting in the captain's office adjourned. Stanley went straight to the lounge, running out immediately asking, "Where's the boy?"

"While you were in the meeting," the desk sergeant answered defensively, "an agent from the FBI, Watson was his name, came in and got the kid."

Stanley turned to his captain, "It *couldn't* have been Watson, Captain. I told you I just talked to him on the phone! He was still in D.C."

"Calm down, Stanley," the officer warned. "The guy showed his badge, his papers were in order and his car was a Bureau issue. If it wasn't Watson, who was it?"

Howard arrived about twenty minutes later. They had to work fast.

"If they're heading back to D.C." Stanley concluded, "they'll probably take 240 because it's a road that's sheltered on both sides by trees."

Howard offered the use of the Bureau chopper. "We'll find him," he assured the rookie.

Stanley replied that he wanted to accompany him; he wanted to make sure the boy was all right. The captain agreed to let him go, with Howard's consent.

The two officers had been in the air about fifteen minutes when they spotted the sedan. It was moving at a rate of at least 80 mph, leaving dust clouds behind. The driver in the sedan, glimpsing sight of the helicopter, lowered his window, took his gun out of his shoulder holster and shot at the helicopter. He knew Howard wouldn't shoot back because Mark was visible in the front seat beside him.

A second man seated in the backseat also fired a barrage of ammunition at the helicopter. A bullet hit the engine of the bird.

"Oh shit!" Howard yelled.

Smoke quickly filled the sky.

The warning lights flashed on the instrument panel, and fear gripped Jim Stanley. *Was the damned thing going to crash?*

The two men in the car below grinned at each other. They knew the chopper's engine was hit and was spinning out of control. Stanley shouted over the noise, "Man, what the hell are we gonna do now?" His voice was filled with panic.

Howard's mind was racing. "I've got to get control of this baby. Just hang on!"

The sedan had slowed to 70, then 65, believing that the helicopter was no longer a threat. About three miles up ahead the men in the car could see that the trees were becoming fewer in number and that the car was about to travel up a steep hill. As the car crested the hill, the chopper, about five feet off the ground, was waiting for them.

The driver slammed on the brakes to keep from hitting the helicopter, and the car skidded off the pavement and became stuck in the soft shoulder. Five Maryland State Police cars seemed to appear out of the cracks of the highway, converging on the sedan. The twelve officers, including Watson and Stanley—who were still in the helicopter—all had their revolvers drawn as the two men got out of the car with their hands up.

Throughout this ordeal, Mark had remained calm. He was bewildered, but he stayed calm.

As the officers apprehended the two men, one of the men handed an officer a piece of paper and told him, "Call this number regarding our arrest." Minutes later the helicopter set down and Howard and Stanley ran under the whirling blades to greet the boy as he merged from the sedan.

"Mark!" Howard shouted.

"Yes," he answered softly.

"I'm Howard Watson," the man said. "Do you remember me? I was a friend of your dad's." He grabbed the boy and hugged him vigorously. "We're going home, Mark!"

He looked at Mark's soiled, bloody clothing; his bandaged feet and hands and felt the boy needed an emotional lift. "More good news, Mark. Your mother's alive!"

"Are you sure? Are you sure?" He grabbed Howard's arm excitedly. "She's okay? My mom's okay?" Tears began to roll down his brown cheeks and he wiped his nose on the sleeve of his filthy jacket. With all his courage, he was still a child.

Howard embraced the boy in a bear hug and Mark buried his face in the big man's shoulder.

"I'm so glad she's alive," he whispered. "I thought I

was all alone." He then grabbed Jim Stanley and hugged him, too.

Stanley nodded to Howard. "Good thing that was a twin-engine bird . . . not that I was afraid or anything." The two men looked at each other and laughed.

As the three of them headed toward the helicopter, one of the Maryland State Troopers handed Howard the piece of paper from the arrested man. Howard glanced at the paper, balled it up, and threw it on the ground.

6

They arrived at Linda Frazier's house and the sight of her grandson made her knees buckle. She just sat and stared at him. The grandmother lovingly kissed Howard and told him that she was in his debt forever. "I was only paying part of the debt I owed to John," he admitted. He also told her not to get too excited. "We still have to wait until Carol's out of the hospital to find out what the hell's going on."

Linda wasn't listening. She was looking at Mark's clothing and noticed his leg, feet and hands were heavily bandaged. "My God, what happened to you? We have to let your Uncle Milton look at you, boy!"

Howard told her that medics in Maryland had taken care of Mark and that he would be fine. He just needed to stay off his feet for a few days. He then handed her vials of various medications for the boy.

Mark wanted to go see his mother, but his grandma told him that they couldn't see her until the next day. Howard commented that the two agents in Columbus were in custody and the prosecutor needed Carol's, and possibly Mark's, testimony to actually put them away for a while.

While Howard chatted with Linda, her other two sons, Bill and Ron, had arrived. Bill swooped Mark up with one arm as he and Ron hugged the boy excitedly. Linda then sent Mark upstairs to take a relaxing hot bath. Once the boy had left the room, Howard recounted the week's emotional toll. He informed the family that they needed to be strong at this point because they were going to be inundated by reporters, so they had better get used to having very little privacy for some time. With that, he returned to his office and gathered members of the Frazier clan exhaled for the first time in over two months.

On his way to the bathroom Mark passed the room that used to be his mother's. He sat down on her bed, picked up one of the fluffy pillows and hugged it softly. He closed his eyes for a moment, then went in to the hot relaxing bath waiting for him.

Dr. Janelle walked out of surgery with good news. Although Carol had suffered a penetrating wound where the lung was punctured and blood entered the chest cavity, she was hopeful. Howard wanted to know if Carol would be in any condition to testify in court in a couple of weeks. Dr. Janelle said she could be in the hospital three or four weeks and then would require about three months' recuperation, but proper rest and a good mental attitude would make her as good as new.

"Yes, Mr. Watson," she said, slightly perturbed, "she'll be able to testify in a couple of weeks, as long as you remember that she won't have a lot of energy, and as long as her testimony doesn't become too taxing on her health."

Satisfied, Howard made two phone calls: one to the FBI Bureau Chief, and the other to the D.A.'s office.

The next day Mark and his Uncle Ron went to the hospital. Linda was thoroughly exhausted and Milton, the older brother, suggested that she stay home and visit with Carol another day. Of course she protested, but Milton's advice prevailed as usual when it came to his mother's health.

Mark and Ron arrived at the hospital and were told

that Carol was still in the intensive care unit and that they could stay only five minutes at a time. When Mark peered into the window of the intensive care room, it seemed to him that his mother was connected to all sorts of tubes running everywhere. It scared him, but his uncle reassured him that they were necessary to keep her alive. He remembered then that she was indeed alive and that made him feel better. When he stood next to her bed and touched her hand, he took a deep breath in order not to cry. Ron put his hands on his nephew's shoulders and massaged them.

Carol's eyes opened slightly. "Mark?" she asked tiredly.

"Yes, Mom," he replied.

She closed her eyes again. The nurse consoled him. "She's fine, honey, tired, but fine . . . she just came through a serious operation, but she's going to be all right. She just needs a lot of rest, that's all."

Mark was told that he would be able to talk with his mother in a couple of days. He and his uncle went home to tell the rest of the family the great news. As he assisted Mark up the front steps of his mother's house, Ron asked his nephew, "How are your feet holding up, buddy?"

"Terrible," he replied.

When Howard returned to his office, he and the Bureau Chief discussed the case up to the point of the missing tape. All they had to go on was the information that John had given the tape to either Carol or Mark, although both Howard and the chief were certain that neither one of them knew they had it.

"Where the hell could Mason have put it?" the chief asked.

Howard knew that asking Carol was out of the question. She was still heavily sedated and wouldn't be able to talk for at least a couple of days. Besides, the hospital staff was not permitting any line of questioning while she was in intensive care. So all he had to go on was Mark's recollection of his traumatic experience. He decided once again to look through the duffel bag, but was disappointed when he couldn't find anything that even remotely resembled a clue.

Mark told Howard how he had thrown the duffel bag into the driver's face, and how he now felt responsible for his mother being shot. "Your mother would have preferred her over you," Howard said to the boy. "You did the right thing, Mark."

After a few weeks, Mark and Howard had become friends. Howard liked taking Mark to the various landmarks in D.C., and Mark enjoyed going. He had soon forgotten that he missed Chicago. His favorite place to visit was the Smithsonian Institute, but he liked the zoo, as well, because it had giant pandas. On this particular day, Mark asked to see FBI headquarters, and Howard obliged. After touring the Pentagon, they had lunch and returned to Howard's office, which overlooked the Potomac River.

It was time to ask Mark if he knew anything about the tape. He said, "No . . . you know, that was the same question those guys kept asking me and Mom."

"Your father told me that either you or your mother would have the tape for me," Howard divulged.

The boy shook his head. "The only two things my dad gave me were his duffel bag and his baseball glove."

Howard had been standing at his window and gazing down one floor below toward the Potomac River. He turned around quickly and asked, "You mean the one your grandfather gave your dad?"

"Yes."

"You have that glove, son?"

Mark again said yes.

"Could we go home and take a look at it?" Howard asked hurriedly.

He nodded. Howard remembered that John's father, Will, had played baseball in the Old Negro Leagues in the 1930s. He knew what the glove meant to John after Will had died. He believed he knew what the glove meant to Mark.

Howard anxiously drove the boy home and performed a visual scan of the glove before taking it down to the lab at the Bureau. After promising Mark that he would try not to deface the glove, he left. When he reached his office he felt around in the glove for any kind of sign from John, but all he came up with was lint embedded in the palm section.

Tim Yamamoto, considered a topnotch pro in the field of X-ray techniques (both laser and radiation), was in the Scientific Laboratory as Howard entered. He told Howard it was going to take about ten time-consuming minutes to go over the glove with the Albascanner. "But," the scientist said, "if anything's in the glove, we'll find it." Howard remained in the lab to watch.

The Albascanner traveled slowly, but thoroughly, over the fingers of the glove. A long ten minutes had passed when the scanner's green light clicked on. A square object, the size of a man's thumbnail, was embedded in the thumb of the glove. "That's it!" Howard shouted.

Tim took a penknife and cut a tiny incision in the glove. With a pair of tweezers he removed a minuscule cassette tape. Thirty minutes were spent in locating the special recorder in the lab that allowed them to listen to the tape—*but the tape was blank.*

Howard couldn't believe it.

"This can't be for real," he shouted. "John told me that his information would be on this tape!"

Tim couldn't believe it, either. Howard Watson, "Mr. Cool" to all the staff, had apparently lost his cool. Tim beckoned across the hall to his new assistant, Ahmad Waverly, and asked if he knew John Mason and anything about his work in the Chicago lab. Ahmad had recently been transferred from the Chicago office and had known John quite well. He told Tim that the Chicago lab had been working on frequency alteration equipment and suggested that perhaps John had had the frequencies altered on the tape so that they fell outside the human hearing range.

"John had this tape made in a lab," Ahmad said to Howard, "and the frequency was converted to something above twenty kilohertz. Human ears can't hear it. So if the tape was found by the wrong person, he, or she, would think it was blank."

When Ahmad paused, Tim broke in with "Good grief, Howard, this tape is like a Gordian knot."

Howard looked confused.

"*You* know," Tim continued, "it's like trying to find a simple solution to a complicated problem. This tape is going to require a special converter because we don't know how to step down the frequency."

Tim took note of Howard's look of disappointment and added, "But we'll try. John must've made a converter and put it somewhere safe. And if he did, man, you'd better find the damn thing before someone else does."

Traveling back and forth to Linda Frazier's house for the past few weeks had started to become routine to Howard and Carol's family. This time he had to question everyone, including Mark, about the tape. No one knew anything about a tape.

"Although John had been in D.C. a month before his death," Bill spoke up, "he didn't mention anything relating to any Bureau business. But then, I was out of town on a case for two of the four days he was here."

Ron, who was also in the house, suddenly recalled something. "John was adamant about Mom baking her award-winning cherry pie for Mark when he visited. He hung around the kitchen while she baked it. It was like he knew that he wouldn't be around anymore to see the preparation. Kinda eerie, now that I think about it."

"Yes, he was really itchy about something," Milton added. Howard listened carefully and filed it all in his head for future reference.

He returned to the lab to consult with Tim Yamamoto again, well aware that he was working on a deadline to find the converter. Tim further mentioned to him that the type of converter John most likely used was an earpiece, because he wouldn't have been aware of the newer generations of frequency converters, especially since the most technically advanced ones were just now being perfected for use in the laboratories. "I'd say the easiest kind for him to have made was probably in the form of an earphone."

Howard went once again to Linda Frazier's house and everyone, including Mark, searched the house for every type of earphone conceivable. Although they found six earphones, none of them fit the cassette deck. "There's gotta be something else," Howard said reluctantly.

"Carol is supposed to be released from the hospital on Saturday or Sunday," Linda said, changing the subject. "If all goes well then we'll have a family dinner on Monday night. Is that all right with your schedule, Howard?"

He was taken aback. He thought the invitation was gracious and he accepted immediately. He felt very excited about meeting Carol, "Finally, after all these years." In the meantime, he was spending the majority of his time at the lab, in his chief's office, and in the District Attorney's office, on a daily basis.

Howard received information through the wire that the State of Ohio was preparing for trial against FBI Agents David Snell and Eric Glenn in three weeks. The state attorney's office in Columbus wanted to confer with him as soon as possible about the case. He had asked Bill Frazier, who had become Carol's legal representative, to travel with him to Columbus the following Monday. Bill agreed.

The cassette tape was locked away in a safety deposit box and Howard possessed the only key. He felt reasonably sure that nothing was going to happen now that an investigation was being conducted.

7

Dr. Janelle had moved Carol to a private room equipped with a telephone. When she had regained the necessary amount of strength to eat solid foods, she was allowed to receive phone calls. Her first call was from Howard. As he didn't want to tax her physically, he tried asking only questions that needed a "yes" or "no" response regarding her shooting. Days later she was able to tell him on the phone that the agents she and Mark rode with were looking for some kind of tape they said John was supposed to have had. Carol felt sure that John had been killed so that whatever information was on the tape would not be known. Howard was now certain that neither Carol nor Mark realized they had the tape. He told her he would visit her as soon as she was physically able to go home.

Carol's family visited often. Dr. Janelle was impressed by her rapid recovery. She felt it was due to the fact that Mark had been found, and in good condition. "You'd be surprised what loved ones, especially children, can do for seriously ill patients," Dr. Janelle said. "Carol will be released on Sunday."

Having been told by the nursing staff to take it easy for the next couple of weeks, Carol replied vehemently, "I'm only thirty-four years old! You people are treating me like I'm an old lady!" Linda Frazier, who was just walking into the room, retorted, "Are you talking about me, young lady?"

Mother and daughter laughed. Linda suddenly realized she hadn't laughed for quite some time, and when she reflected on her relief, she started laughing again. Carol realized she had been in this hospital for over three weeks and was more than ready to leave. Her long frame had been in bed long enough, she thought. She gazed in the bathroom mirror. She quickly looked behind her *knowing* that the person in the mirror was not her. Having worn no makeup in weeks seemed to make her chiseled features appear worn—and the look made her want to puke. Her hair looked a fright and her freckles seemed to stand at attention. Although everyone who visited Carol said she looked beautiful, she felt somewhat vain. Never mind that the color was finally returning to her medium brown complexion, she thought, or that her soft cow-like eyes were beginning to take on a more cheerful look than before.

"I look awful!" she screamed. "But, I am alive and I'm going home!"

Two days passed and Howard had not found the listening device for the tape deck, though he still continued to look. He pulled himself off all other supervisory matters to concentrate solely on John Mason's case. Albeit the chief wanted to add other agents, Howard was able to dissuade him, but only for a while, as the chief gave him a deadline to come up with concrete information. The chief's main concern was that Howard might get too close to the case to look at it objectively. Howard agreed to the possibility. There were times in his ten-year career that he, too, had had to take an emotionally involved agent off a case. Howard was the first to admit that he was "involved," so he knew he had to work fast and he had to work efficiently.

Privately the chief mentioned to his wife that he wanted this case resolved quickly, because he didn't want Howard going off the deep end trying to resolve it.

"Howard is one of my best supervising agents," he told her, "and I can't afford to lose him."

Howard left the office and started walking toward his car. His stride was always slow, but steady. He'd learned in Vietnam that to be in a hurry increased his chances of stepping on a mine, so he had learned to walk slowly and carefully. Today, because he felt the weight of the case on his shoulders, his walk was even slower than usual. He felt somehow endangered by this case and, he thought, *If I were to die, who would be affected by my death?* At thirty-six, he was still unmarried. He had no child to carry on his name, and everyone close to him lived in New York. He suddenly felt alone.

Howard had gone to Vietnam against the wishes of his fiancée. Susan hadn't wanted him to enlist, and had refused to talk to him for three days. She knew when he had been accepted to the Academy that he would be trained for Vietnam, but she hadn't realized until the day he said "I'm going to 'Nam," that the reality of the statement stung unmercifully. He understood how she felt, but he had a bigger picture in mind. He wanted to do his time in 'Nam, work for a couple of years in a federal government position, probably utilizing his fluency in the Russian language, and then join the FBI. He was informed that the Bureau regarded an applicant with military experience highly on the preliminary application. He had his career all mapped out, but he wanted Susan in his plans, too. It took almost a year to convince her but she never felt it was the best decision, and Howard again understood. He loved her but he was committed to his plans. She was his best friend and he cared for her deeply, but Vietnam was something he had to do.

As it turned out, they eventually broke off the engagement with relief on both sides. Vietnam had changed them. She had been against the war even before Howard had enlisted. She wanted a house, kids and a man who worked a 9-to-5 job. He eventually wanted to "earn a seat" with the FBI. It just hadn't worked out.

1975: FBI Academy, Quantico, Virginia

J. Edgar Hoover had been dead three years to the day when Howard walked across the carpeting of the three-year-old FBI Academy building. Hoover had enjoyed 48 years of authoritarian rule and Howard's father, George (and other non-white Americans) was glad to see him gone. George had mentioned on several occasions that "only death will get Hoover outta that chair." Howard smiled, thinking back on his father's words. His father had been right, he thought. Hoover's reign ended only with his death.

After being approved by the New Agent Review Board, Howard entered the FBI New Agents Class #75-05. In four short, but grueling, months he would become proficient in weapons training; he would be engaged in the various methods of scientific crime detection, attend 645 hours of classes, become expert in Russian interpretation, and develop competence in seeking out activities affecting internal security.

While thumbing through the numerous training manuals, he came to the realization that the 16 weeks of training were going to be his "hell on earth." Nevertheless, he retained the fact that *eighty percent* of new entrants make it through the training and, remembering this, sighed with relief, acutely aware that he would be one of the "eighty percent."

The evening before Howard's first day of classes found him arranging his dorm room, books, toiletries and memorabilia. The room quickly reminded him of his West Point days. Nestled in the woods of Quantico, Virginia, and situated on a United States Marine Corps base, the 385 wooded acres of land made Howard reflect on different times. Times before Vietnam and West Point—and Susan. Although he was only 26 years old, the reflections made him feel old. That night was the only night he slept lightly. He was up early the next morning, ate breakfast in the Dining Hall, and headed quickly to the "Building." The mission on the glass doors energized him. "To lead and inspire. . . . To influence change and forge partnerships."

After reporting to the Director of New Agents, he was informed that all new trainees had been divided into teams. Before he could locate his name on the list, a familiar finger tapped him on the shoulder. It was John Mason, whose name was connected to his on the list. Howard could not remember the last time he was this happy.

This mood changed quickly during **HELL WEEK**.

The first week in the Academy was all about stamina, stamina, and stamina. Howard was so exhausted each night that he couldn't find the energy to finish his dinner, read his mail (forget about answering it), or return phone messages from family and friends.

Eventually the week was over.

The next three weeks focused on investigative matters within the Bureau's jurisdiction. Classroom work found him immersed in subjects like sabotage, organized crime, kidnapping, bombing, and rules of evidence. Scientific Laboratory work dealt with bullet markings, hairs and fibers, paint flecks, heel prints, dynamite wrappers, tire treads, headlight lenses, and rope samples.

The next four weeks dealt solely with endurance. The

science lab became painfully draining. The firearms training required knowing *completely* the use of revolvers, shotguns, machine guns, and defensive tactics. The library, because it was open 24 hours a day, became his "home away from home."

In his thirteenth week, weaponry and physical training started to gel. Even classroom work became somewhat easier as terms like "infrared" and "ultraviolet spectrophotometers" and "x-ray diffractometers" rolled off Howard's tongue almost effortlessly—enough to scare his parents.

The last three weeks were review, review, and review. Working as a team solidified his bond with John Mason in a way he could not have foreseen. John became his "brother," and although Howard was the younger of the two, he deemed himself John's "protector," telling him on graduation day, "I will absolutely, from this day forward, move heaven and earth to protect you, should you need me." John simply smiled and hugged him.

Howard impatiently brushed away the reflections and grimaced. *Why wasn't I around for him? Why wasn't I here? Why didn't I protect him?* He pounded the desk with his fist. He had to figure out this case and bust it wide open.

On Sunday, he had gone to play basketball with guys he knew from the DC Fire Department. He enjoyed staying in shape, thus he played with the men once a week in the nearby neighborhood park.

He was unaware of a young man sitting in a car across the street, watching him and his friends shoot the hoops. The man watched for about five minutes, then drove off slowly.

Just as Howard's intense workout began, it ended. He had suddenly remembered that he wanted to surprise Mark at dinner Monday night with his dad's army duffel bag. He knew he wouldn't be in the office on Monday because he was flying to Columbus early in the morning, so he felt now would be as good a time as any to pick up the bag. He assured his buddies that he would join them another time, but right now he had to run an errand.

He entered the FBI Headquarters building, put his "Special Agent" card in the slot in the lobby door, and simultaneously stood in front of a camera as the monitor above read "HOWARD LOUIS WATSON." The door clicked and he entered. In the next lobby he was greeted with a large picture frame stating three words: "Fidelity, Bravery, Integrity"—the FBI oath. He stared at it for a moment, then proceeded to the next door where a computer-generated voice asked him to put his thumb on the glass. Seconds later the door clicked and he slid in. He waved to a Federal Security Guard as he entered the hallway.

Nearing his office he noticed a faint light coming from beneath the door. The light was moving, as if being carried. Howard drew his revolver from its leg holster and opened the door slowly. The man who had, minutes earlier, watched him play basketball was searching frantically through the drawers of his file cabinets. The office was in disarray. Howard asked abruptly, "What are you looking for?"

The man looked up, shocked at Howard's appearance, but noticed quickly that he was blocking the only exit from the room. In one quick motion, he picked up a chair, threw it through the draped window and jumped out, taking broken glass with him in his shoulder. *How did he get into my office?* Howard thought. More importantly, he knew the intruder had been looking for something specific. He also knew that he had to find that converter!

Howard dealt with Security, but gave only information

that was obvious and got out of there with the duffel bag as quickly as he could.

Carol was coming home. She'd been in the hospital almost a month and she couldn't wait to get home. She was nervous, though, about meeting Howard. For the past couple of weeks all she heard from Mark was, "Howard took me here," and "Howard took me there," or "Howard taught me how to play basketball." Mark certainly liked Howard. She wondered if she would, too.

On Monday at 7:00 P.M., after a long day in Columbus, Howard arrived at the Frazier residence. Howard was stunned by Carol's beauty. They talked about Vietnam, the FBI Academy and other, many, memories of John. He apologized profusely about not making it to John's wake, and for not being by her side while she was going through the ordeal of packing and getting to D.C. She repeatedly assured him that she understood, and that his being on assignment in another country, especially Russia, had to be difficult for him too.

Howard had seen a dozen snapshots of Mark through the years, and only a couple of pictures of Carol, but he had always thought she was pretty. Today, however, he felt an urge for her that surprised him. He was slightly embarrassed in feeling the way he did. He thought it best to sit elsewhere at the dinner table.

Dinner was almost too cheerful. Everyone, including Mark, wanted to know what was going on in the case, but all were too polite to broach the subject. Finally, Carol couldn't stand it any longer. "I'll be glad when this nightmare is over," she blurted.

Howard resisted the temptation to tell her about the ransacking of his office for fear it might shake the family.

He also felt it was Bureau business and wanted to keep it that way.

Hoping to appease her, he mentioned that it was only a coincidence that the plane she and Mark were to have boarded in Chicago had exploded. The FAA had discovered a malfunction in one of the engines. But the fact that the explosion had nothing to do with John, or Mark, or her, did little to soothe Carol.

The doorbell rang and Milton left the table to answer the door. Five reporters were gathered at the door with questions for Carol regarding her release from the hospital, the trauma she suffered in Columbus, Ohio, John's possible murder, and any and all questions regarding Mark's impossible trip, by foot, to D.C.

Milton gestured quickly to Bill who rose from the table to join his brother at the door. Bill said to the press, "Mrs. Mason is resting comfortably and recuperation will be accelerated if the press will allow her and our family privacy for at least a couple of weeks." Howard meanwhile was staring at Carol as her brother talked to the press. She was looking at him too and smiled. The members of the media slowly and reluctantly descended the steps of the porch.

The two men returned to the dinner table where the conversation for the next half-hour revolved around "the audacity of the press."

Mark could hardly wait for dessert. He had gobbled up his dinner and sat waiting impatiently for everyone else to finish. When dessert finally arrived, he wanted to have the first piece of cherry pie, which made everyone laugh. Howard looked puzzled. "No one in their right mind would dare take the first piece of Mom's cherry pie, except Mark," Ron said laughingly.

When Mark cut a large piece for himself, his mother exclaimed, "Mark, you can't possibly eat all that pie!"

But Mark wanted to try anyway. He cut small pieces for everyone else and Linda Frazier said she was certainly glad she had baked a cake, too.

After stabbing the pie with his fork for a few seconds, Mark suddenly asked, "What's this?"

Everyone looked puzzled, except for Howard. It had finally dawned on him.

Without explaining, he moved around the table to Mark. "Sorry, young man, but I really have to do this."

As he stabbed the pie in several places with Mark's fork, he asked Linda if she had "recently baked this pie?"

"No," she said. "This is a pie I baked when John visited us a couple of months ago. As a matter of fact, I was about to throw it out because it had been in my freezer longer than I care to remember, but Mark begged me not to."

Suddenly a white stringy material appeared and a smile crept onto Howard's face. He grinned like a boy who had just received a bike for his birthday. He pulled the earpiece out of the pie and exclaimed, "This is it!"

The group stared blankly, as if hypnotized by the strange discovery. Carol seemed more lost than the rest of the group. Bill broke the silence at last. "I knew John was creative, but I didn't realize how much."

"Howard," Carol asked him directly, "is this earpiece in any way related to John's death?" He nodded and shrugged his shoulder, "Maybe" as he walked to the kitchen sink and began cleaning the earpiece under running water. Ron followed him and broke in excitedly, "This was the reason John wanted Mom to bake a pie, because it gave him the perfect opportunity to put the earphone in the pie as it was baking! Knowing Mark's craving for cherry pie, he could count on it being only a matter of time before we found the earpiece. How come it didn't melt, Howard?"

For the next fifteen or twenty minutes the family discussed the case and felt encouraged for the first time. Perhaps the end was around the corner. Howard reiterated his plea for them not to press him for any specific details, as Bill could answer many of their questions. He did promise, however, that they would be the first to know when the case broke, first even before the media.

After expressing his thanks for dinner and dessert, he had to leave. It had been an extremely long day and he was tired. Carol walked him to the door. She was disappointed to see him go, but she tried to hide her feelings because she wasn't ready to admit to herself how much she was attracted to him.

At the door Howard turned toward her. "Would you and Mark be available for dinner? As soon as you're up to it, of course." Carol was startled, but quickly recovered.

"That sounds wonderful, Howard," she said hiding her joy. "Thank you for thinking of us."

She slowly closed the door and turned around to stares from her family. Her brothers were grinning and nodding to one another, much to her annoyance. "It's only dinner!" she said defensively as she walked past them on her way to her bedroom.

When he reached his house, Howard called Tim Yamamoto. Tim couldn't believe it. "I'll bet John is upstairs laughing up a storm this very moment."

Howard couldn't agree. "I'll bet he was wondering if we would ever find it, Tim. He hid it pretty good, I have to admit." Neither he nor Tim wanted to wait until the next morning to find out what was on the tape, but they knew they had to. They didn't know whom to trust at this point, especially if they showed up at the lab at 11:00 P.M.

On Tuesday morning, Howard rose early, showered,

and grabbed a bottle of orange juice from the refrigerator, before he dashed out the door.

Tim Yamamoto's wife was just getting up to shower when Tim appeared fully dressed, a donut in his mouth, a cup of tea in one hand and the morning paper in the other. "Gotta go, Kel," he mumbled through the donut. "There's an emergency down at the lab. See ya later!" With that, he was gone. Kelly Yamamoto tried not to look curious—but she was.

The men drove up to their designated parking spaces at the same time. Howard fought with mixed emotions, relief and disappointment. Although the tape meant they would unravel possibly all of the mysteries surrounding John's death, it would also most certainly put the blame on someone Howard—and possibly Tim— knew. It was too late for Howard to feel sympathy for another agent. A person had been killed and it had been his buddy.

As Tim was connecting the earphone to the cassette deck, a noise sounded across the hall. Both men stiffened. It was Ahmad Waverly. Tim quickly motioned to him to hurry into the office and then, to feel less paranoid, locked the door behind him. He turned on the tape. What they heard was frightening. They each knew the information it contained would be big, because an agent had been killed for it, but they soon found out that it was bigger than just John Mason's death.

8

My name is Carl Sunderland. [said a baritone voice on the tape] I was a helicopter Crew Chief with the United States Army from June 1972 until May 1980. I was responsible for the repair and maintenance of the "birds." I was paid $200,000 to sabotage the helicopters in the transport planes that would have rescued the Iranian hostages in April 1980. I was PROMISED no deaths. The accident was supposed to abort the rescue attempt only, but eight people were killed!

The reason I'm giving you this information, Mr. Mason, is because I'm dying of cancer and I know it's because my conscience has eaten me alive. [pause] Mr. Mason, I have documented proof that two former CIA operatives, two senators of the United States, and three defense contractor CEO's, paid and directed me to sabotage the rescue mission. I also have copies of bank statements that reflect four fifty-thousand-dollar wire transfers to my bank account—paid to me for rigging the "birds." I'm not proud of what I did, but I want you to have the proof to take those bastards down. I deserve the punishment I'm getting and I know it.

Howard turned off the tape. He looked at Tim and Ahmad and told them that "Carl Sunderland's body was the one police identified from the explosion that happened about four months ago in Chicago." Howard now felt sure this tape was valid.

They returned to the tape . . .

January, 1980, I was approached by two CIA operatives in Chicago. Their names were Carlton Veaux and James Vanderwal. They told me that my family would be taken care of financially, if I mechanically sabotaged two helicopters that were going to Iran. Well, I said no at first, and when I was told repeatedly that no one would get killed, I thought that it wasn't a bad way to make two hundred grand, and besides, no one would get killed! They paid me two hundred thousand dollars not to ask any questions, and so I didn't. I put all of the money in an investment account under a false name, and each month the interest is wired into my ex-wife's account to supplement her teaching salary and our two kids. I told her not to ask any questions. I'm telling you all this because I'm no longer afraid that something will happen to me, I know it will. It's just a matter of time.

When the mechanic brought me the maintenance and safety forms to sign that said the helicopters were in flying condition, I signed them, but kept the papers. Once the "birds" were loaded onto the transport planes to take them to the desert in Iran, I was supposed to check the oil in the transmission of one bird and add about a quart of sand to the oil. The oil wasn't visible to the pilot, if he decided to check it himself, and since we were going to be over a desert, the crew wouldn't know that the sand didn't come from the desert. That's what happened to the first helicopter, and the engine quit on its way up.

On the second "bird" I drilled a small hole all the way into one of the hydraulic lines because I knew that, under pressure, the hydraulic line would become useless. Later, when I went back to the bird, I exchanged the flexible line with one that I'd had material failure on another helicopter and that I had saved for this mission. I knew that when the line was analyzed they would find that it was a natural defect in the material and they would never know that the helicopter was sabotaged.

Unfortunately, the next day in the States I heard that the mission had been scrubbed. I was told that eight men were killed and five were seriously injured. That's when I decided to keep the directives I was given by the two operatives for future use, just in case they tried to pin the accident on me. I guess the senators who called themselves "Leopold and Loeb" became nervous and afraid that I would talk, so they decided to tell me why they paid me to sabotage the birds "for the sake of the United States."

Three days later I was picked up by Veaux and Vanderwal. I taped a tiny recorder to the inside of my high-top gymshoes, and used a special secret listening device, like the one you're listening on, and was driven to a place near Lake Michigan. I can't tell you exactly where it was, because they blindfolded me when they took me to talk with "Leopold and Loeb," but I could smell the lake. When we got there, I was searched for anything that might prove embarrassing to the senators later, but they didn't search my shoes. I don't know exactly who Leopold and Loeb were because I remained blindfolded the whole time. But I do have their voices on tape if you decide to check out my story. I activated the tape recorder by crossing my ankles when I sat down . . .

[a pause in the recording, and then Sunderland continued . . .]

Located in locker number 1949 at the Union Station downtown, you'll find a metal box containing all the information I've described. You'll also find the tape-recorded conversation between the two senators, the two CIA operatives and me. Mr. Mason, I have a feeling I won't live long enough to help you with this mess, but take care of business, brother, because I was told you are the man. And take care of yourself; you just might need it.

The three men sat motionless for what seemed like forever. Howard finally broke the silence. "The chief must hear this!"

When the Bureau Chief arrived several hours later, Howard went into his office and closed the door behind him. He then let his boss hear the tape.

"You've got to go to Chicago and get in that locker, Howard," the chief said. "I want you to take the first thing smokin' outta here . . . and, Howard?"

"Yeah, Chief?"

"Watch your back."

Howard called Carol Mason and told her that he had listened to the tape, but, unfortunately, couldn't discuss it with her. He then called her brother Bill and told him that he had found a break in the case of John Mason's death. Bill felt encouraged. He assumed that Bill would call Carol and they could discuss the matter (what little they really knew) further. But Carol was annoyed that Howard couldn't give her any more information. "What is going on?" she wanted to know.

Bill assured her that she would be the first to know whatever news Howard came up with. "Just be patient a little longer, Sis," he said. "Howard's working on something big and he will get back to you, I promise."

Once his flight arrangements were made, Howard reluctantly gave the listening devices to his chief who told him the exhibits would be locked away. Howard felt he had no choice but to believe what he had been told.

The next morning he caught an early flight to Chicago. He detested early flights because they interrupted his sleep. He had reached a point in this case where it was getting to him and he really needed sleep to get him through this mess.

He was relieved that his flight was an uneventful one.

After arriving at Chicago's O'Hare Airport, he caught a cab to the Union Station downtown. On the way he began to think how his image of Chicago had changed. It was now, in his mind, a busy and callous city. "The city where John was killed," he said to no one.

He arrived at Union Station and headed straight to the security office, believing protocol would benefit his efforts. The Head of Security was at lunch, so for the next twenty minutes Howard had time to reminisce about the reasons he had become an FBI agent.

1964: Brooklyn, New York:

"But, Dad, the FBI doesn't turn away Negroes," fifteen-year-old Howard was telling his father. "Negroes for some strange reason just don't apply to the Bureau."

He was a student in high school when he decided he wanted to work for the FBI. His class had been studying the John F. Kennedy assassination, the year before, and the FBI had impressed him considerably with its professionalism and degree of intelligence. His father couldn't understand why a black person, especially *his* son, would want to work for an arrogant, white, elitist group like the FBI. Howard didn't agree with that assessment. He felt that minorities had been afraid to apply to the Bureau. He also felt if you were going to change negative opinions of a group, you had to *know* about the group to change it.

Howard and his father, George, were always at opposite ends of the totem pole when it came to politics and vocations. Howard understood, though, his father's attitude toward J. Edgar Hoover and Hoover's known policies toward Negroes—specifically his father's hero, Dr. Martin Luther King, Jr. George told his son on several occasions

70

that it was a "well-known" fact that Hoover had become angry with Dr. King for criticizing the FBI. Hoover then retaliated, according to George, by bugging and wiretapping Dr. King's life.

February, 1967

He had desperately wanted to attend the United States Military Academy at West Point but when he realized that his excellent grades were only a portion of the requirements, he became depressed. West Point's policy of admitting well-rounded, academically superior students was not unlike other well-established colleges, but admittance to West Point required that Howard had to be referred by an elected official in his community, like his senator or congressman. Even after being recommended, Howard found he still wasn't guaranteed an appointment. An official could only refer twelve people to the academy from his state each year and of these twelve, the "Point" took two students (maybe). "West Point is a difficult place for anyone to get into," Howard told his parents.

George Watson had been a very good friend of the congressman from New York, but the time-consuming part was getting in touch with him. George tried for two months, starting in December, to no avail. Finally, when Howard had received two full academic scholarships to other schools and was about to give up his plans to attend West Point, the congressman contacted George. Two weeks after sending copies of Howard's grades, basketball and tennis accomplishments, and ROTC recommendations to the congressman, the man called George to say he'd be honored to refer Howard to the Academy. Seven days later a certified letter requesting an interview arrived from West Point.

Actually, George enjoyed the idea of his only son going his own way. Howard was independent and intelligent. He was athletic, like George, but he had his mother's common sense. Anne Watson was a smart woman. She was designated "the person in the family who separated the fights in the Watson household." In reality, Howard and his father didn't fight much. His two younger sisters fought more with their dad than he did. But his vocation choice was not his dad's, and would never become his dad's. From the age of fifteen until he assumed his role as a FBI agent, Howard's father would never be happy. George wanted Howard to pursue a "safe" career, like medicine or engineering.

Howard and his parents had driven to upstate New York for the interview. Howard had never been more nervous in his life. His mustache, which he'd had for only three months and had sworn never to shave, had fallen to the razor for this occasion. Even George was nervous. Howard could tell because his father always bit his lower lip when he was nervous, and that's what he did all the way to the Academy.

The telegram arrived one week later. Howard had been admitted to West Point's Cadet Summer Training.

September, 1967

The campus impressed him, as did upstate New York. Howard's room looked very reserved. He shared it with three other cadets and was informed by administration personnel that room changing three times a year was not unusual at all. The rifle racks above the beds were used for

72

the endless number of parades in which he would participate during the next four years.

Looking north from his room, he had a picturesque view of the large hills rolling into the Hudson River and Constitution Island. Nestled in the hills were the mess hall and the cadet barracks. Although in the minority, Howard was of the conviction that the food at the Cadet Mess was really good. He was always amazed that all 3,500 Corps of Cadets ate at the same time and were served at their tables. "What service," he would often say.

In the distance, he could barely make out the field artillery sheds and the two statues: one of George Washington on a horse, and the other of Sylvanus Thayer, the "father of the military," so called because he was the first Director of the Academy. There were endless old cannons and statues, and the lush greenery seemed to make the air more humid, "more so than even Brooklyn, New York." When Howard strained his eyes to look south, he could see the large field everyone called the "Plain."

West Point was a gray, granite-looking place and Howard was required to wear a uniform at all times—but he rather enjoyed this. He knew that when his five-year commitment to the Point was over, he would have to serve in Vietnam, and there was a good chance he would be a captain. His degrees would be in Criminal Justice and Russian, and he would work for the Federal Government, then enter the FBI Academy. He had carefully planned his career. At the official pinning ceremony following graduation he had become a second lieutenant. He had graduated in the top 5 percent of his class and felt he had done his best. His father felt the same.

When he volunteered for early duty in Vietnam, though, his father was furious. "This ain't our fight!" George told his son. "This is the white man's M-O, always getting into another country's business when they're fighting against themselves! You don't need to be getting into the middle of this mess, Howard! Ain't a Vietnamese alive who's done us wrong! Enough is enough!"

Howard's mother was very sad at the news. But she felt Howard was going to do what Howard wanted to do, regardless of the people around him who had other ideas for his life.

9

October, 1972: Tong San Nut, Vietnam

When he stepped off the transport plane in the country of Vietnam, a blast of hot air hit Howard in the face. The place felt like the inside of a furnace. The country was not at all like he thought it would be. Vietnam was beautiful, true, but it didn't come close to being a paradise. The greenery was the greenest he'd ever seen, glistening and somehow threatening. What scared Howard, though, was the strange smell in the air. He later found out, to his horror, that it was the stench of death.

"Lieutenant Watson, sir!"

A Specialist Fourth Class saluted him and brought him to stiff attention. "Sir, I'm to take your bags to Post B and set you up there. Please follow me, sir."

Howard nodded at the young man and waited while he gathered the bags. The thought of calling the Spec a "young man" suddenly struck Howard as funny, and he laughed inwardly. The Spec was younger than Howard, no doubt, but Howard himself was only twenty-three. He walked behind the Spec for about one hundred yards until they reached the tent, which housed the commanding officer. After receiving his instructions and meeting other officers in the camp, he arrived at the tent where he would be quartered. The Spec shouted, "Sir, your home for the next seven months, sir!"

Howard smiled, returned the salute and entered the tent.

Inside were two other lieutenants unpacking their clothing. The first man, a Latino, Howard figured to be 5'11" and 185 pounds. His name was Louis Castro. He'd graduated from New Mexico State University the previous year and had enlisted in the Army to pursue tactical weapons engineering. Louis told Howard that he was to be in this hellhole for the next nine months. They talked for a couple of minutes and then Howard resumed unpacking.

The second guy, a black man, was 6'4" and weighed about 200 pounds. He had graduated from the Northwestern University Law School in May, and, like Howard, had enlisted for Vietnam so he could qualify as a candidate for the FBI Academy. Howard felt an immediate affinity for this man, John Mason.

The first realization of war came to Howard two weeks later. It was 2 A.M. and he'd been sleeping.

"A soldier's been shot! A soldier's been shot!" someone was yelling outside his tent.

The next thing Howard heard was gunfire, lots of it. Days later he pieced together the story of a Vietnamese woman and her two kids who'd been showing up at the camp for some time. For reasons Howard was unable to discover, the woman suddenly had opened fire on an American GI and shot him in the back. She and her kids tried to run, but every soldier on duty had opened fire on them. Howard had mourned for the children. His honeymoon in Vietnam was over, and he knew that he, too, might die here.

Five weeks before Howard was to be shipped out of 'Nam and back to the States, the compound was attacked. He and John Mason, who had become close buddies during their tour of duty, were returning to their tent one evening when Louis Castro motioned to them to "Get down! Get down!" In a flash, the shells were falling all around them. Four tents, including theirs, were hit. Suddenly Louis started screaming, "I've been hit! I've been hit!" The agony in his voice was terrifying, but they couldn't get to him through the rain of mortar fire. John began to work his way toward the tent, which had collapsed on top of the wounded Castro, inching his way across the ground on his belly.

As soon as he reached Louis, John saw that the man had been hit in both legs by shrapnel and was unable to stand up. John struggled with the tangle of canvas and Castro's weight for several seconds, until he remembered his duffel bag. He dived under the tent and came up with the bag. Shifting the weight of the bag to his left hand, he grabbed Louis's shirt with his right and began dragging the wounded man on the duffel bag away from the target area. They were almost clear of the shelling when a mortar exploded right in front of them. A hot pain seared John's left thigh and his leg buckled under him. As he fell, he realized with surprise that he'd been hit. Suddenly Howard and two other men were at his side dragging both of the men to safety.

Once out of the firing, an army medic assessed the damage to John's leg, which required a tetanus shot and a few bandages. John grinned at Howard, "I'll be damned if that duffel bag didn't save my life AGAIN. If I hadn't been holding it in front of me, that shell would've splattered all over my leg."

Howard smiled nervously. "Man, you and that bag are too much!"

Louis, under heavy sedation, called to John. "Thank you, John, for trying to save my life. You are my friend." With that, Louis lapsed into unconscious.

77

John looked at Howard. "What does he mean TRYING to save his life? If it hadn't been for me . . ."

Howard laughed and shook his head. John realized how silly he sounded and laughed too.

Louis Castro was shipped back to the States several days later. Howard and John learned that he had lost both legs. Howard also learned months later after leaving the military, through a phone call from Louis's wife, that Louis had committed suicide. He agonized over whether to attend Louis's funeral, but in the end, he was there; so was John. . . .

The security chief, who had returned from lunch, brought Howard back to the present. He asked Howard to show his badge and identification. Howard told him that he needed to get into locker number 1949 and that he had papers authorizing him to take whatever was in the locker. The chief perused Howard's papers with the FBI seal on them and told a security employee to open the locker.

Inside the locker was a locked metal box the size of a cigar box. A combination lock was built into the box, but there was no sign of a combination. Howard searched the locker thoroughly, but couldn't come up with anything that could be used as a combination. As a last resort, he took the floor out of the locker. Taped to the underside of the floor panel was a piece of paper wrapped in plastic. "Amazing what you can learn from television," he remarked to the security man. The paper contained a printed combination.

Howard opened the box and quickly, but thoroughly, eyed the papers and the cassette tape. He closed the box and thanked the security people for their help. Using the phone in the security office, he called his chief in D.C.

"I've got it," he said.

"Good work. Are you coming back today?"

"Oh, hell yes!" Howard replied, and hung up.

He decided against visiting the Chicago headquarters. Although he was quite friendly with a lot of agents in Chicago, he thought it wise not to show his face, at least not until this case was settled.

A cab, parked outside the train station, pulled up in front of Howard as he exited the building. He entered the cab and told the driver "O'Hare Airport, please." While he viewed Chicago's numerous skyscrapers, he was unaware that the driver had slowly removed a gun from the inside of his jacket pocket and laid it on his lap. Howard *had* noticed, though, that the redheaded driver looked nothing like his Middle Eastern identification photo on the dashboard.

As he moved slowly in his seat to try to position himself behind the driver, he simultaneously removed his gun from its leg holster with his other foot. In a split second the cab driver had turned down a side street and stopped the car. He opened the money window, turned around to Howard with his gun pointing in Howard's face and said, "I need that box you've got, Mr. Watson."

Howard immediately slammed the money window on the driver's wrist, knocking his gun to the floor. He then jumped from the car and ran through high-rise building after high-rise building until he concluded it would be a miracle if the driver caught up with him. He was alarmed by the surprise attempt to scare him, so to thwart any further chance of being caught off-guard, he called a colleague at the FBI Chicago office.

Phil Davenport, an FBI agent with the Chicago office, had been a friend of Howard's and John's since the Quantico days. The men went immediately to a bar. After downing a couple drinks each and reminiscing about the past decade in the FBI, they spent the next two hours trying to figure out the possible reasons for John Mason's murder.

They had none. As it soon became late, Phil suggested to Howard that he stay with him and his family for the night. Howard was too tired to refuse.

The next morning, Howard shared a pleasant breakfast with the Davenport family and was driven, this time, to Midway Airport.

At Midway, Howard flashed his FBI badge and identification card to the airport security to be spared the lengthy line at the gate. He boarded the plane and took a seat in the last row. When his flight landed at JFK Airport in New York City, Tim Yamamoto was there to pick him up. They drove the four hours to D.C. together where they discussed nonstop, who, besides Howard's Bureau Chief, knew Howard would be at the train station in Chicago?

At headquarters Howard asked Tim to join him and the chief in the chief's office. Inside the box were papers directing Carl Sunderland to sabotage two of the helicopters that were being sent to Iran to rescue the American hostages in April of 1980. Sunderland had been too smart for his own good, Howard thought. He'd made copies of the "orders" before the operatives could burn them. Also included in the box were four bank statements reflecting wire transfers in the amount of $50,000 each.

Lastly, there was the cassette tape. It was the same size tape that Sunderland had sent to John Mason. Obviously Sunderland knew what he was doing—or did he? Tim put the cassette tape in the deck but nothing happened, no sound at all. When they didn't hear anything for a full two minutes, Howard started wondering if this tape was a higher frequency than the other tape. Before he could ask, the chief had glanced over at the outlet and noticed the plug had fallen out of the wall socket. All three chuckled nervously. The tape played . . .

Sunderland's voice:	Why the hell am I here?
"Leopold's" voice:	We've decided to tell you about the mishap in Iran because we thought you'd want to know that you were doing something for the good of your country.
Sunderland:	What could I have been doing for my country that caused folks to get killed, and others to get hurt?
"Loeb's" voice:	Mr. Sunderland, it was an accident.
Sunderland:	You're not gonna try to pin this shit on me, are you?
"Loeb's" voice:	No, sir, we're not, but we do have something to say—hear us clearly and well.
Veaux:	We want you to know, Carl, that this information is highly confidential and should it leak, you will be held accountable. We won't recognize your existence, do you understand?
Sunderland:	(with a caustic laugh) I was wondering when this little conversation was gonna take place.
Vanderwal:	Hell, we don't want to do this, but you've left us with no choice! If you talk, we'll deny it. You'll be found out as a bad boy who dropped out of the Army because he couldn't go along with the program. You could go to jail for military theft, manslaughter, vandalism, and a score of other things. [pause] Should I go on? [short pause]

Sunderland:	No.
"Leopold's" voice:	We've paid you royally, haven't we, Carl? So you won't want to talk?
Sunderland:	[shouting] WHY THE HELL HAVE YOU BROUGHT ME HERE? [dull sound of something hitting something]
"Loeb's" voice:	Please don't raise your voice again, Mr. Sunderland. (sound of moaning)
Sunderland:	[taking deep breaths as he talks] You assholes don't know what you've done! You killed eight people, you seriously wounded others. My God, one guy is permanently disabled! You harmed those hostages. They could have been killed, too, you bastards!
"Leopold's" voice:	You knew they weren't going to be rescued when you took the money, Carl.
Sunderland:	But I didn't know anyone was gonna be killed!
Vanderwal:	It was an accident, man! One helicopter was coming down to land, are you listening to me? It hit a plane carrying live ammo and they both blew. [pause] We're not going over this again.

Sunderland:	I can't get over this. You assholes have such a low opinion of life. What do you do, stay awake all night dreaming up ways of getting rid of people?
Veaux:	Let's not try to be such a good guy, Carl.
"Loeb's" voice:	I think we've told you enough, Mr. Sunderland. We hope you keep your mouth shut, and of course we'll do the same. Are we clear?
Sunderland:	You've made yourself very clear . . . sir!
"Loeb's" voice:	By the way . . . [the tape ends].

Howard and Tim sat silent. Tim heard his pulse as it pounded in his ear. "It can't be possible," the chief said, breaking the silence. "But then I'd look like a fool if I didn't believe this. We're selling the United States to a bunch of outlaw legislators. We're gonna have to go slowly on this, boys, because it's the *goddamn CIA!* Let's get the Attorney General on the line."

The next three months tested Howard's mettle like no other time in his life. While waiting for a cab one morning, he was almost run over by a pickup truck that didn't stop. Washington agents who were colleagues of David Snell and Eric Glenn constantly asked him if the stories they were hearing were true. The press, the attorney general's office, his friends and neighbors, some of whom he'd never seen before in his life, all steadily bombarded Howard.

Mark and Carol performed admirably in Columbus, Ohio court. Mark successfully made the jury understand the anguish and horror he had felt at the hands of Agents Snell and, especially, Glenn, who shot his mother. He also (without inducement) told the jury that he felt responsible for not protecting his mother more than he did. There wasn't a dry eye among the jury members.

10

On the same day that the CIA operatives were being arraigned in Maryland for conspiracy, murder, and other charges, Carol and Mark were appearing on several television shows, including *CNN, Good Morning America* and *Oprah*. After eight long months of trials, testimonies, and the press, mother and son had been given the "go-ahead" nod by their attorneys that they were free to take back their lives. Since it was spring break, Carol decided *now* was the time. She and Mark busily packed for a trip to Jamaica. Their cab pulled up.

In Columbus, Ohio, FBI agents David Snell and Eric Glenn were waiting for the jury to return with its verdict. Because of Carol's testimony, they knew their chances for acquittal were slim.

As the cab neared the airport, Carol reminisced about the past twelve months and how she and Mark had miraculously gotten through them.

CIA operatives Carlton Veaux and James Vanderwal sat motionless in the Maryland courtroom. They, also, were waiting for a jury's verdict. Neither man looked worried, as they had constantly been assured by their attorneys that the jury would probably find them "not guilty" on the more serious charges, thinking this was part of the CIA's operation.

However, the Attorney General had competently explained the CIA's job description, because the jury returned a verdict of "guilty" on all counts. This included impersonation of an agent acting for the Bureau; kidnapping across a state line; and collaborating in a conspiracy against the United States Government.

Veaux became catatonic. His attorneys were busy talking to him, and although he heard the word "appeal," he felt he had no chance in hell of overturning the court's decision. Vanderwal absorbed the verdict differently. He immediately told the attorneys that he wanted to appeal the decision. One week later both men received sentences of four years in federal prison. Two days later, Veaux was found dead in his cell from an apparent self-inflicted gunshot wound to the head.

As Carol and Mark checked their baggage they found that, due to an earlier flight not arriving on time, their flight would be forty-five minutes late. Carol recalled the last time they were at an airport together. She shuddered. It seemed forever ago.

David Snell's knees buckled as he stood and faced the jury foreman. "Your Honor, we the jury, find the defendant David Snell *guilty* of criminal attempt to commit a felony." (Kidnapping through false pretenses.)

Eric Glenn's smile faded as he faced his peers. "Your Honor, we the jury, find the defendant Eric Glenn *guilty* of criminal attempt to commit a felony, and assault with a deadly weapon." (For shooting Carol Mason.)

Michael Morris was jumpy. The jury was returning.

"Your Honor, we the jury, find the defendant Michael Morris *guilty* of manslaughter in the first degree (he confessed to planting the explosive device in Carl Sunderland's car). The jury foreman continued. "We also find the defendant *guilty* of vehicular homicide." (Through eyewitness testimony, Morris was driving the van that had caused John Mason's car to go off the road.) He received fourteen years for planting a device that ultimately caused a death, and four years for vehicular homicide.

Roger Glass, a convicted petty thief, had ransacked Howard's office. Although he left no fingerprints on the chair he had thrown out the window, he was fingered by Howard and the two ER nurses at the Medical Center who attended to his shoulder wound after he jumped from Howard's window. He received two years in federal prison.

Carol felt justifiably happy as she, Mark and Howard walked toward their gate. Although John was dead, and although for over a year their lives had been a total nightmare, she and Mark were fine. He was doing well in his new school, and she was attending law school at night. In the daytime, she had a job tutoring U.S. Government employees' children. Howard had helped with this. As a matter of fact, she thought, if it hadn't been for Howard's help, she and Mark would never have known that John went to his death a hero. She breathed a sigh of relief. The confirmation of what she'd known all along, that John was a good guy, made her grateful to God. She was grateful, too, that Howard Watson was in their lives.

Yes, Howard, she thought. It was a relationship that started with meaning. She and Mark liked Howard very much and felt certain he liked them as much, or more. As a matter of fact, he was paying for their trip to Jamaica.

Howard had explained to her that although *he* couldn't pinpoint concretely, who "Leopold and Loeb" were, his superiors had an idea. "Unfortunately, indictments aren't based on ideas," he told her. "They're based on probable cause and facts." He said that through

candid testimony, FBI Agents Glenn and Snell had informed the U.S. Attorney's office (in exchange for lighter sentences), that two CIA operatives, Veaux and Vanderwal, hired them.

Two senators who went by the sobriquets of "Leopold and Loeb" hired Veaux and Vanderwal. "L&L" represented three defense contractor CEOs to make sure the Iranian rescue mission was botched. Of course Veaux is now dead, and Vanderwal won't name names, but the probability of senators from Arizona, Colorado, Nebraska and/or Texas is high, since those are big defense contract states. The Bureau will be doing an in-depth look at these senators.

Howard continued. "Snell said that in 1980 these companies wanted to see the U.S. a power again, and to *them* that meant a greater buildup of defense hardware. Pres. Carter's administration at that time, according to Snell, was weakening American military might around the world. It was not in favor of stepping up arms contracts, which meant billions of possible dollars to these companies. The administration was made to look silly and incompetent. Snell also said that Veaux and Vanderwal had leaked information about the President's brother to the media. The story said the President's brother was selling arms to the Libyans. They capped it off by creating a technical mishap in Iran. Snell said the idea was to make Americans feel (and they did) that they had no confidence in an Administration that was incompetent, and couldn't pull off a rescue

88

attempt in the middle of the night in a desert. It was The Bay of Pigs all over again."

Carol looked stunned. "I thought Carter was the person who *sent* the CIA to Iran in the first place to arrange the hostages escape? You're going to tell me that they stabbed him in the back?"

"Yes, Carol," Howard said reluctantly. He continued slowly, "Snell even admitted that the President might have pulled off the rescue if the CIA hadn't intervened. He had a good plan. Unfortunately the defense contractors who bought those senators didn't want a rescue, and so it didn't happen. These companies required a new administration—one that was in favor of boosting arms, and boosting dollars to their coffers."

"How did the CIA get so much power?" Carol demanded. "Who is supposed to govern *them?*"

"The President is supposed to," Howard chimed in. "Nelson told me in the U.S. Attorney's Office that the CIA employed secret efforts to influence *numerous* events abroad.

"Although I hate to admit this, because the FBI has been *clearly* wrong in certain covert operations—but even "Watergate," which revealed widespread wrong-doing by the FBI, was *partly engineered* by former *CIA* employees."

Reading the *Brunswick Gazette* one morning prompted Clara Baumgarten to call her daughter. "Sally," she said excitedly in the phone, "it's that little boy! Remember the little kid I told you slept here about a year ago? Well, he made it to Washington. Lord, am I happy!"

Jacob Tryer and his family were just sitting down to breakfast when his son George yelled from another room, "Pop, please, come and see the television. That little black kid's on it!" Jacob peered at the television as if staring at a ghost. "My God, if I'da know'd that little boy was bein' chased, I'da helped him more'n I did." He looked happily at his wife. "Course, it looks to me he had the Lord's help, I'd say." They returned to the breakfast table.

Agnes Mobley had been astonished when she heard the voice on the phone say, "This is Mark." A week later she and her husband, and her two sons met Mark and Carol for dinner in D.C. Carol tried repaying the forty dollars Agnes had given Mark at the bus station in Monessen, but Agnes refused the money, saying she was just thankful that Mark made it home in one piece.

Carol glanced over at her son who would be turning eleven in a couple of weeks. She never wanted him to forget that if it hadn't been for his courage and his love for his father, it would have been impossible to solve this case.

Every publication from *Time* to *Newsweek* to *Ebony Magazine* had carried an article about Mark. Mark's friends thought he was "the coolest." Mark was feeling good about himself, too. This was what Carol Mason wanted for her son—peace of mind.

They walked to their gate. She looked back and waved at Howard. She didn't know why, but at that very moment she felt the nightmare was over.

Howard arrived at the FBI Headquarters building and stared at the Service Martyr Wall in the foyer of the lobby. A new face had been added. Albeit Howard knew and understood a new face meant another new hero, it also meant that another FBI Special Agent had been killed in the line of duty.

The new face belonged to John Mason.